ELEMENTAL
KIDNAPPING

ELEMENTAL KIDNAPPING

Elemental Kingdoms

Horace Mom,
keep your dreams
alive!

Bridget Tolle

BRIDGET TOLLE

TATE PUBLISHING
AND ENTERPRISES, LLC

Published by Tate Publishing & Enterprises, LLC
127 E. Trade Center Terrace | Mustang, Oklahoma 73064 USA
1.888.361.9473 | www.tatepublishing.com

Tate Publishing is committed to excellence in the publishing industry. The company reflects the philosophy established by the founders, based on Psalm 68:11,
"The Lord gave the word and great was the company of those who published it."

Book design copyright © 2016 by Tate Publishing, LLC. All rights reserved.
Cover design by Albert Ceasar Compay
Interior design by Jomar Ouano

Published in the United States of America

ISBN: 978-1-68187-517-0
1. Fiction / Action & Adventure
2. Fiction / Fantasy / General
16.01.08

For God, who got me to where I am today.

PROLOGUE
TWELVE YEARS AGO

"Jigu! Jigu!" she ran about the castle, shouting.

The castle looked like a giant mushroom. Most wouldn't even call it a castle, but to the Earth Kingdom, it was gorgeous. The mushroom had doors and windows all over. It was accented with vines and flowers. The whole thing looked like a garden exploded.

"What is it, Chikyū, darling?" he asked. The Earth king was sitting at his desk. The inside of the mushroom castle was similar to a garden as well. The floors were grass and dirt. The furniture was made from live trees that grew there. Nature was everywhere and had created (with help from the Earth people) the entire home.

"I've had a grand idea!" exclaimed Chikyū. She was always excited when she came up with a new idea. The entire kingdom benefited from her many great decisions.

Jigu put away his work; it could be done later. His wife was here in this moment, and he needed to focus on her.

One of the things all the kingdoms thought similarly about was marriage. The parents would pick a bride or groom to marry their heir. The heir would then agree; there were never arguments. The two would get married, and both would have their names changed. Every king and queen had to have a name connected to the meaning of their kingdom element. After the marriage, the two would become one. The two ruled the kingdom together by consulting one another in all matters. The king and queen were equal.

"What is this idea you've had?" he asked.

"I was just in touch with Mizu, Kasai, and Kūki."

Mizu, the Water queen; Kasai, the Fire queen; Kūki, the Air queen; and Chikyū, the Earth queen would meet up on very, very rare occasions to talk about the kingdoms and how they were doing, usually this happened during the spring when the Air Kingdom was willing. Chikyū always wanted to meet up, but they knew what could happen if the kingdoms became one again.

"And," Chikyū continued, "I found out that we all have daughters! It's really funny because they were all born the same year. Isn't that crazy? And Kūki has twin girls! It sounds so exciting. Anyway, I thought that all the girls should get together and see if they like each other. Wouldn't that be wonderful? Just think of how our little Petunia would get along with all of them! She'd make such great friends since she's so outgoing and loving."

Jigu smiled, though not for long. He did think it was a wonderful idea. Maybe the kingdoms could become one again because of the bond their daughters made at such a young age.

But he knew what it could cause. He knew that the Fire Kingdom wouldn't want to. He knew that half of the time, the Air Kingdom wouldn't want to either. He wished they *could* do it, but he knew that if they did…

"Chikyū, dear," he started, "I wish we could do that, I really do, it's just that…well, you know. We can't. You know what might happen."

"Oh," she replied, saddened. "Yes. I suppose I do." She put a smile back on her face. "Well, you get back to work, and I shall as well!"

She turned on her heel and left. Chikyū wanted the kingdoms to get together and become one. She knew that they could live in harmony if only they tried. Right now they didn't even trade with each other! She desperately wanted to be close to the other queens, but they didn't seem to want to be close to her.

She sighed.

Hwajae and Kasai laughed. They were in a secret room in their castle. The castle was akin to a colossal construction of volcanic rock constantly consumed by licking flames.

This particular room resembled the structure of a sauna. Everywhere in the castle felt like being close to flames.

Although the residents of the Fire Kingdom didn't notice the heat surrounded them, it was comfortable. The hotter it was, the more comfortable they were.

"She-She wanted our daughters to meet up!" exclaimed Kasai in the midst of her laughter. "C-can you believe that? It's ludicrous!"

"I know!" Hwajae added, picking up their very young daughter, Pyra. "Did she seriously think we'd hand over our little girl over that easily?"

"Who knows?" Kasai's laughter diminished. "Have you responded to Djamar yet?"

"No."

Djamar was in charge of the Fire Kingdom's military. He had suggested to King Hwajae the military go explore some nearby land. It didn't appear to be a part of any of the Four Kingdoms—the common term for the Fire Kingdom, Air Kingdom, Water Kingdom, and Earth Kingdom. Since it was land, it definitely wasn't part of the Water Kingdom or the Air Kingdom; it wasn't covered in plants like the ones seen in the Earth Kingdom, and it was not covered in volcanic ash like the Fire Kingdom was. Djamar thought it would be a useful place to train the military as well as a good safe haven in times of trouble or if another war came up. King Hwajae didn't know what to make of it.

Queen Kasai noticed their daughter had fallen asleep.

"Well," Kasai said, "it appears Pyra should be set in her flames to sleep. I'll take her, so you may have time to think about this matter with Djamar. We'll discuss it together later."

With that, she scooped up her precious child and took her to Pyra's room. Kasai sealed the walls of flames around her daughter's fire bed. She knew as well as anyone else the only way a child would learn to control fire was to constantly live with it. Eventually, her daughter would learn to exit her room by commanding the flames herself. For now, Pyra usually became furious with the walls.

One day, Kasai foresaw, *my child will become the best fire commander this kingdom has ever seen. She will rule this land with the help of her husband. She will become one of the greatest rulers this kingdom has ever seen. No one will dare contradict her. Her immense power will allow her reign to last.*

Adjusting from the vision, as the Fire Kingdom's people do, Kasai continued to walk down the hallway. She walked underneath the castle that was a volcano. Peering into the lava, she pondered upon the vision she just received.

Her thoughts veered to the kingdom as a whole. She recalled the tour she had taken at the beginning of her and Hwajae's reign.

One day, she tried to mind-speak to her daughter, like those from the Water Kingdom. *This entire kingdom will be yours.* She tried to send the images in her head. She hoped for her daughter to have the best dreams she had ever had.

∞◡∞

This all happened in spring. It was a happy time for the Air Kingdom. Everyone was joyous and glad. Their attitudes toward the world allowed the kingdom to flourish this time every year. So of course, Gong-Gi and Kūki were excited. The entire kingdom was happy, and that meant the towns would be prospering.

Of course, this was only because it was spring. If it was summer, the citizens would be egotistical and cocky. In the fall, the citizens were depressed, and practically nothing was done. When winter came, they were all harsh to one another. Spring would proceed to follow, and the cycle would continue.

The queen and king were in good spirits when they responded to Chikyū. They immediately wrote a letter in reply saying, "Yes, we'd love for our daughters to meet! It sounds like a great idea. When would be the best time?"

However, Chikyū sadly declined. She noted they all knew what their daughters' friendship could lead to. Kūki and Gong-Gi realized it too and would be sad as well, if only it were fall. Alas, the married couple was not able to be melancholy for it was spring.

They responded again. Their good attitude poured out into the letter. They said, "Maybe it won't happen like last time. Maybe this time, it will be different. There might not be another war. We know what had happened; how could we not remember what generations past have said? If only we tried, we could find out and see!"

Chikyū confided in Jigu, although she already knew what he would say. Having the gift of wisdom, they replied, "No, the kingdoms mustn't repeat history." With that, the matter was closed.

Gong-Gi and Kūki were slightly disheartened, but they looked toward the future for hope. One day, the kingdoms could come together again. They could only hope and dream on their clouds, for that was what they were best at in this season.

The entire kingdom lived in the clouds. The buildings were made up of clouds but were quite solid. Most of the buildings were domes since the Air people tended to drift toward circular objects. They disliked hard, sudden angles. The castle was a giant sphere that floated above the bottom level of clouds. At the moment, the clouds reflected a prismatic bright light. It became brighter as summer ensued but would darken as the kingdom approached winter. The Air people wore no shoes, but neither did the other kingdoms. In fact, whenever the Air people walked, little clouds would pop up and stay, unless they were on solid ground. The feet clouds could not survive in a different atmosphere and would dissipate.

One day, as they sat on the clouds in their kingdom, Gong-Gi said, smiling at Kūki's beauty, "Wife, isn't it a lovely day about?"

"Why wouldn't it be, husband?" she queried.

"Hm…" He thought. "Maybe because I haven't had the chance to be with you until now. We've both been so busy with the kingdom. Everyone seems to be at their peak like usual. Our kingdom is thriving! We've also been busy with our daughters. It seems they're quite the handful!"

Kūki laughed, and soon enough, Gong-Gi joined her. Several of the castle workers passed by but didn't consider that the two rulers of the kingdom appearing off-task could possibly be unusual.

Their identical twin daughters, Cirrus and Stratus, ran into the room while Kūki and Gong-Gi were laughing.

"What are you laughing at?" they asked innocently.

Each parent picked one up and placed her in their respective laps.

"It was something your father said," Kūki replied. "And may I ask who is who today?"

The children shook their heads. They were often switching their names around. It was fun to confuse the castle workers.

"Nope!"

Most of the time, the rulers of the Water Kingdom could be found reading the minds of others. All in the Water Kingdom had this gift, so it wasn't anything new or surprising when another would speak to someone through mind waves. However, usually the ones who were trained in this ability can only touch the minds of those at the edge of his or her city.

These citizens did not always use this ability for "the greater good," as they were taught. Out of all the kingdoms, this gift was one of the easier ones to use against others. In addition on how to read others' minds, most of the citizens were taught how to block such things. This was also the only gift where the people were forced to make a counterability.

However, sometimes the rulers would read the minds of their fellow queens and kings.

Mul and Mizu, the Water king and queen, pondered upon everything that had happened. They'd been watching and listening to the other kings and queens. They knew they probably shouldn't, but it was the fastest way for them to receive information.

The people of the Water Kingdom lived underwater. They had gills on their necks rather than lungs in their bodies, and the castle was made out of coral. Fish and other sea creatures swam in and out of it, minding their own business. It was a bright kingdom as well, but rather in a different way. Rather than the light's reflection being bright, the buildings were many different colors. This was due to it being made of coral and was the only thing that unified the buildings in the Water Kingdom. Their shapes varied greatly. The first queen and king made it so in the beginning since all of the original monarchs created their castles. The villagers' homes were based off of the castle in that kingdom. This was true in all four kingdoms.

"Well, these are an interesting turn of events, aren't they?" ventured Mul.

"Very," agreed Mizu. "What are your thoughts?"

Mul and Mizu opened their eyes as one.

"I say we should do as Jigu said and not get our daughters together. But the other kingdoms were silly in their reactions. It's a…fair idea, but we all know the possible consequences. Besides, I don't want our Currentide going around those crazy people from the other kingdoms. I don't want them tainting her brain with their thoughts. She's too shy for that kind of socialization."

Mizu nodded. "I say we wait and see what fate has in store for our daughters. We should allow them to take their own paths, to find their own way in life. We shouldn't force them upon a course, especially at this young of an age. Maybe when they're older…"

When the five princesses, Petunia, Pyra, Cirrus and Stratus, and Currentide grew older, fate had something in store for them their parents could never have imagined.

1

Air

The season was summer. It was time for the brash to come out. At least, for the Air Kingdom, it was. The cockiest of all's coronation day was at the end of the year, which meant this kingdom better get ready for Princess Stratus, also known as Princess Cirrus, to become queen. Her parents weren't entirely sure which twin she was, so they called her by both names. It wasn't that they forgot; they just simply didn't know. She was fine with both names and found it perfectly right for her twin to be remembered. She was the daughter of Queen Kūki and King Gong-Gi.

Most of the year, her light-gray hair cascaded down. It wrapped around her thighs and body. Her dress had long, bubbly sleeves, each having a long slit. She had a thick sash around her waist. The dress cut away at the bottom of the sash, like a moth's wings. Under it was a tight skirt. The dress was a pretty silver. She walked barefoot, like all the others in the Air Kingdom. Her skin was fair in color. Her nails were white, along with her lips. Her almost white irises were wispy and seemed not at all there if it weren't for a darker gray ring around them.

"Who's next, huh?" Stratus challenged.

Cirrus was playing one of the games with her cousins who had invited some commoners. They were all very competitive at this time of year. They had similar outfits and characteristics to Stratus, more or less elaborate.

The game involved flying in the wind and seeing who could race the track the fastest. Sometimes tournaments were created, but that was not the case today. Today, they were simply messing around. It was always fun for the others if they could beat the princess. However, it would be a lot easier were she not so exceptional.

"I'll accept your challenge," said a new voice.

Stratus hadn't seen him before. He was obviously a commoner, Cirrus could tell that much. The others seemed shocked he had showed up. They whispered quietly to each other about "the legendary flyer." She crossed her arms, unimpressed. She could easily beat him.

"With the exception," he continued, "that we have terms. I want the chance to get something out of this."

"Fine. Choose the terms. I don't care."

He smirked. "When I win, you have to tell us which twin you are."

Cirrus's smile turned into a frown. Everyone in the kingdom knew this was a touchy subject, especially for Stratus. Whoever this kid was, he wasn't afraid to push people's buttons. Well, it was summer.

"Fine," She couldn't show weakness. "And when I win, you have to tell me your name. For now, a nickname will suffice. I'd at least like to know a name of whomever I am going up against, so when I win, I can shove it back in your face."

His grin broadened. "Deal. Feel free to call me 'The Best Flyer You've Ever Met.'"

Stratus made a *tch* sound as she assumed the position. The Best Flyer She'd Ever Met assumed his as well. Cirrus's cousin Markus became the referee.

"On your mark!" he shouted.

They tensed in their positions.

"Get set!"

They breathed out and mentally prepared themselves.

"Go!"

They were off. They were neck and neck on the track, but it was only the beginning. They still had 276 yards left to go. It could be anyone's game at any point.

They came upon their first turn and managed it well. It was sharp and quick, so Stratus hadn't expected her opponent to conquer it as easily as she. She knew now she must raise her expectations of him for now. However, there was still time left for him to mess up.

Their next turn came and went, quicker than the first. Cirrus pictured a map of the track in her head. They would be going straight for a while until the largest and longest turn of the entire track. It scaled upward, thus also making it the hardest. The turn would bring them above the rest of the track. After that, the final turn brought them back to the starting line. This was her favorite part, since it sloped downward. It was a great moment where she could rush to the finish and usually defeat her opponent. She had easily memorized this track as a child. She was the heir to the Air Kingdom after all.

They remained side by side until the final slope. Stratus could do it; she was in the final stretch. She gained speed and laughed as she passed The Best Flyer She'd Ever Met. Ha! So much for *that* title. Maybe he should change it to—

It became his turn to pass her. She desperately wanted to wipe that smirk off his face. No, he couldn't beat her. She had a reputation to uphold. Pride got to the best of her as she tried to surge forward. Dismay fell upon her face when she realized he was too far forward, and she didn't have enough energy or power to beat him.

The commoners cheered for The Best Flyer They'd Ever Met as he passed the finish line. Cirrus refused to be a good sport. The Best Flyer She'd Ever Met's hands were on his hips and a wide smirk played upon his lips. His arms opened out as he spoke.

"So," he said, "I won." He crossed his arms. "Now, tell me, we're all dying to know. Which one is your real name? Stratus or Cirrus?"

She sighed, admitting defeat.

"All right, I'll tell you."

She realized by telling him, being the commoner he was, he'd tell anyone and everyone who would listen. Soon enough, the entire kingdom would know. But a deal was a deal.

"My actual name is—"

"Cirrus!"

She turned around. Her maid was running toward her.

"I knew it!" The Best Flyer They'd Ever Met said, pointing accusingly.

Cirrus crossed her arms. She'd known her maid her whole life. She knew what would happen next.

"Is that my real name?" she questioned. One of her eyebrows was raised. She knew when only her maid or butler came, the other would surely follow, and they always called her by a different name.

"Stratus!" called the other voice.

Sure enough, here was her butler, right on time.

"It's an urgent matter!" continued the maid.

"You need to come right away," the butler said.

They turned to leave when The Best Flyer They'd Ever Met interrupted them.

"Wait, wait, wait!" he said. "So which twin are you? We had a deal!"

Stratus's maid pulled on Cirrus's arm. The maid said, "We have to go now! You mustn't be late!"

Her butler and maid proceeded to drag her away.

"I don't know," she yelled in reply to The Best Flyer She'd Ever Met. "Which twin am I?"

She laughed haughtily as he forcefully threw his cap down. Well, he should've challenged her sooner. Princess matters are *very* important. After entering the castle and passing through many hallways, Stratus finally asked the question on her mind.

"So what exactly is this 'urgent matter' I simply *must* attend to?"

Her butler answered monotonously. "As you know, your coronation day is coming up at the beginning of the coming year. Today you are required to decide on multiple things such as what flowers you would like imported, what silverware we should use, et cetera, et cetera."

Cirrus shook her head. She could always count on her butler to make things sound boring. Not that these were interesting matters anyway. Well, it beat telling out her biggest secret.

The process of making decisions was long and tedious, but it must be done. It was a longstanding tradition for the heir to pick everything that would be at his or her coronation day. No one else seemed to care or appreciate it, and that was found to be acceptable.

After the long afternoon of deciding things she didn't care about, Stratus was ready to take a royal nap. The only problem was she had to get ready for that evening where she and her parents would meet with guys around Cirrus's age. Her family would meet and discuss things with each one. She would have to accept whomever her parents chose, and she wouldn't know until the day of her marriage. "Love" between the spouses was not cared about whatsoever when it came to marrying off the heir to the throne. If both parents found the spouse suitable, the spouse and heir would be married, and their names changed.

Stratus did not find tonight enticing. No one would be good enough for her anyway, but what she really minded were the preparations involved. She was to cleanse herself, and then her maid had to help Stratus dress in the fanciful clothing. After that, Cirrus's maid and helpers were to fix up Stratus's hair, the longest task of all. This was the part she hated. Her maid and helpers pondered over what to do for a decade then took even longer to get it perfect. Honestly, Cirrus didn't care. It was hair, and couldn't it simply remain down? Wouldn't that be easiest for everyone?

She sighed as the afternoon turned into evening. Soon, she would get to eat food with a bunch of men she didn't know. Couldn't she pick a random one? As if any of them would be as good of a king as she would be queen.

Finally Stratus's maid declared her finished. "Now," the maid added, "you know no one else could have done a better job, right? I'm the best maid you'll ever have."

Cirrus was taken to the banquet hall. The food was the best any of those being served would ever have, for it was summer, a time to impress. Also, they were in the royal castle, and why wouldn't it be the best food they'd ever had? Here were the best chefs and servers the entire kingdom had to offer.

So Stratus assumed her spot beside her parents. Across from her sat her mother, and beside her was an elder from the council. One day, she would sit where her father sat, which was at the head of the long table. As the other kingdoms were, the most important people sat at the head in order from greatest to least. Many sons of lords came with their fathers or mothers. Cirrus played with her food for most of the meal, occasionally speaking with the elders around her or her parents.

Soon the discussions (more appropriately called interviews) began. Stratus spoke with the son's parents; Cirrus's parents spoke with the potential kings.

The long night continued to drag. Any man from the ages fourteen to eighteen was invited to come to the castle and be interviewed by the parents. Some of her possible in-laws obviously wanted their son to marry for the money, others were incredibly poor. (Too poor for the princess no less! How could they ever afford anything?) And some seemed to want to simply try it out to see if they could possibly marry into royalty. Stratus laughed at all of these parents. How in the world could any of them expect to be good enough to rule an entire kingdom with her anyway?

Finally, the night ended. Cirrus could at last go to floor and sleep. The Air Kingdom didn't sleep on beds since the floor, being clouds, was soft and cushy already. She was released from the fancy clothing, and her hair was let down once more. She put her earlier garb back on and lay down. Knowing she would need some good sleep tonight, she took a drug that allowed her to feel double the amount of hours of sleep she had. It also allowed her to not be awoken by anything until light shone upon her, which was a wonderful thing when one wished to remain undisturbed for a period of time.

Before the drug kicked in, she decided being a princess was hard. No one else understood what it was like to try and have fun, only to be put down by boring decisions and parties. She'd only have a few hours of sleep before another day started. Was ruling the kingdom harder or easier? She could probably rule it better than her parents.

That night, Stratus dreamed about the different ways she would rule the kingdom. Of course, under her rule, the Air Kingdom would thrive and be at its peak.

2

Earth

Petunia rose from her bed, which was formed from the branches of a tree. As she stretched, she looked out her window. It was a beautiful day. She might as well go enjoy it.

Jumping off her bed, she prepared for the day. Her brown hair fell about her shoulders. It had green streaks and was incredibly curly. It was as if cowlicks burst around on every place they could find on her head. Her eyes were leaf green, their texture as if one was looking up into the treetops while standing on the forest floor. She had a heartwarming smile that made anyone feel welcome. Her lips were a tan color, similar to that of her skin. Her nails were a light green. Her attire appeared as that of a peasant, perfect for a disguise. She adorned a beige undershirt with a dark-green vest over it along with a light-brown skirt. Flower stems wrapped around her feet though not from her doing.

She grabbed her basket and cloak and headed out. Sometimes, Petunia liked to go to the town near the castle. In this guise, she was allowed to run errands for some of the busy or elderly who simply didn't have time or couldn't physically.

Today, she thought as she walked. *I'll start at the baker's.* An elderly woman and her granddaughter ran it. The child's mother had her without being married, not that it was the woman's fault. Her mother died during childbirth, and the father was never seen nor heard from again. The child was given to her grandmother and grandfather. Her grandfather was lame and lay sick in bed all day long.

Mrs. DuBois, the owner, was a funny old lady who was not afraid of anyone. It made Petunia laugh. Mrs. DuBois was also a lifelong friend of Petunia's father, King Jigu, husband to Queen Chikyū. Mrs. DuBois's granddaughter was only nine, but even that was old enough to be doing work.

"Hello," greeted Petunia. "Oh my."

Chickens were everywhere in the store. It usually wouldn't have been a problem except they were running wildly and eating all the bread. Celia, Mrs. DuBois's granddaughter, was trying to calm them down, but it was a futile attempt.

Mrs. DuBois's hands rested on her hips. "Can you believe the nerve of some people?"

Petunia set her basket down on the counter. She filled with worry. "What happened, Mrs. DuBois?"

She sighed and explained. "That young farmboy down aways stopped on the road to look at somethin' or other. Well, while he wasn't payin' attention, his chickens got loose. Guess where they headed? Of course, the baker's. Eventually the boy realized his chickens weren't in the cart anymore. I tried tellin' him the chickens were here, and he should come get them before I whack him upside the head!"

Petunia laughed. "Mrs. DuBois, when you told him, were you yelling at him?"

"How else am I s'posed to get my point across?"

"I'll go find him, Mrs. DuBois," she said with a laugh. Grabbing her basket, she headed out.

"And tell him," Mrs. DuBois added, causing Petunia to stop. Mrs. DuBois waved a whisk at her. "Tell him if he doesn't come get them, I'm sendin' them to the butcher's!"

Petunia laughed, promised, and moved on. She walked down to a local farm. She knew exactly which farmboy Mrs. DuBois was talking about. She had complained of many things pertaining to that very farm.

She opened the gate and passed through, closing it behind her. It was like any other farm in the Earth Kingdom. It had plenty of land, filled to the brim with crops. It was easy to grow plants since those of the Earth Kingdom could provide them with more nutrients than required as well as allow them to grow year-round.

Petunia passed by a farmhand.

"Excuse me," she said. "Would you mind telling me where Johnny usually works? I have a message to give him."

The farmhand peered into the horizon.

"Usually he stays by the animals or potatoes. If not, then try in town. It's not my job to keep track of the whereabouts of all of the workers, but we're all happy to help."

"Thank you!"

"You're welcome!"

She continued to walk beside the crops. They were growing very well. Petunia was glad she lived in the Earth Kingdom. It was nice to see plants constantly growing. She was especially glad to be the princess of it and the heir to the throne.

At last, she came to the barn area with animals. After walking around and looking at where she might hide had Mrs. DuBois yelled at her, she found Johnny the farmboy in the stables. He was on the second tier, which was filled with hay. After climbing up she sat near him, careful to keep her distance; she heard him crying.

"Johnny?" she said tentatively. He looked up.

"Did the old lady send you? You aren't going to punish me for the chickens, are you?"

Petunia smiled. "No, I just wanted to talk."

Johnny wiped his face on his sleeve. He couldn't be seen crying in front of a girl, especially an older one at that.

"What did you want to talk about?"

"You're twelve, aren't you?"

He nodded.

"Great! I have a job for you to do if you're up for it. I'll pay you a couple of bronze pieces if you do it, too."

His face lit up. He would have been happy to receive one copper coin. Bronze was high class! Petunia knew if she gave him anything higher, he might be suspected of thievery.

"But first," said Petunia, "I need you to collect the chickens from Mrs. DuBois's bakery."

Johnny's face fell. "You're making me go back there?"

Petunia nodded. "She told me she'd give them to the butcher if you didn't take them."

He became panicked and stood up. "No! She can't do that to them!"

Petunia looked around. "Between you and me," she whispered, "I don't think she was serious."

He looked relieved. She stood with him and said, "She really doesn't want those chickens in there, though. They'll eat up her bread, and she won't get any customers!"

Johnny looked somber but agreed. With that, they headed back over to the baker's. Eventually, after much sighing and confusion, everything was straightened out. Mrs. DuBois and Johnny were somewhat on good terms again. Petunia asked the old lady if she had any more errands to run.

"Well," she said, "now that we're short on bread, I'll need more flour for sure. You know where I get it and what I like." She smiled.

"All right, I'll be back soon."

Petunia proceeded to head out of the baker's, closely followed behind by Johnny.

"Miss!" he said. She turned around. "Miss, what was the job you wanted me to do for you?"

"Oh, I'd nearly forgotten! Pardon me," Petunia exclaimed. "Actually, if you can go run Mrs. DuBois's errand, I think I'll go run mine. I'll still pay you, and you'll probably become on better terms with Mrs. DuBois.

"Now, she's very picky about her flour. You must go to the Hickklebury's farm to retrieve it. Make sure to get exactly three bags filled to the brim. If they spill, Mrs. DuBois believes it to be bad luck, so you might have to get another. Also, bargain with the Hickkleburys. Keep bargaining until you pay three copper coins. Here's the money, plus some extra. Mrs. DuBois likes to receive change. She'll know if you have cheated her, so don't keep any of it for yourself. She'll love you if you get all of this right." Petunia pulled out two bronze pieces. "Here's my payment for running this errand for me. Thanks again!"

With that, she left and headed off for her own errand. She stopped at midstride. She hadn't intended to practice today, but why not? She changed direction and errands. She walked all through town and to the other side before she arrived at her destination. Her new destination was a small shack of which many of the townsfolk went to hone their skills. Petunia liked it simply because she found it wise to have multiple teachers. She found they often taught her different things. As the heir of the Earth Kingdom, she needed to have highly honed skills. It was simply to be expected.

She knocked lightly and quietly. The door creaked open.

"Um, excuse me?" she said. "Mr. Sruli? I don't have an appointment, but I was wondering if you had time to give me a lesson?"

Mr. Sruli had only recently moved into the shack. He'd been there for a couple of years, teaching all who were willing how to use their powers wisely. Of course, wisdom wasn't a hard thing to acquire in the Earth Kingdom, but it never hurt to have more.

Mr. Sruli always seemed to have a five o'clock shadow. He liked to live in the darkness. He was easily kinder than he looked, but still a great teacher. Petunia would almost say he was better than her teacher back at the castle. However, she should say the two were equal for this was the Earth Kingdom, which strived for equality in all things.

Mr. Sruli looked out his sole window. "Well, I have a lesson later today, but I believe I have time for one in between now and then."

"Great! I give you a multitude of thanks."

The two went outside and ventured into the nearby trees. They were very sparse and great for practice and training.

Mr. Sruli went over some basic warm-up exercises with Petunia by barking out the technique names off to the side. She made sure to take deep breaths and concentrate. Plants were very delicate and easily broken. It felt like a sin to destroy nature, so she must always be alert and trying her hardest.

She didn't really need to be taught anything else. She just thought it was a good idea to always be practicing and seeing if there was something new for her to discover. At this point, she could probably be coming up with her own techniques.

"Stop tensing!" Mr. Sruli shouted. "Go with the flow. Do what feels natural. Don't you remember our photosynthesis lesson? Become one with the plants. No, stop!"

Petunia was caught in a trance. Her arms moved as she commanded the plants, but she quickly lost control. Of their own will the plants began wrapping around Petunia tightly. Mr. Sruli backed away and built a cage around Petunia. The plants fought to enter, still in the attack mode Petunia had them in.

Another student of Mr. Sruli came and defeated Petunia's plants. Using his power, Mr. Sruli lifted the cage off of Petunia then picked her up and ran.

Mr. Sruli knew if they had continued to wrap around her, she would have become consumed by them, finally becoming one with the plants as all in the Earth Kingdom wished to happen to them one day. A voice inside had told Mr. Sruli to allow her to live, that her life wasn't supposed to end just yet. He held onto that notion, running to the medic. Maybe the medic could help her. Maybe he could do something Mr. Sruli couldn't to help this poor girl.

One of the problems, however, was Mr. Sruli didn't know Petunia was the princess of the Earth Kingdom, and it was treason to take the princess anywhere without her consent.

3

Water

Currentide floated on the outskirts of a crowd. She was peering into the thoughts of others, careful they didn't take note. She'd occasionally catch her own parents prodding into her thoughts. It slightly annoyed her. She figured if they, King Mul and Queen Mizu, spent their time looking into other people's thoughts then she might as well too, right? One day she would be ruling the Water Kingdom. Shouldn't she be practicing what her parents were already doing?

Currentide's lips were a cold blue. Her hair cascaded around her. It flowed constantly like a stream. It took color of whatever was around it, just like water. Yet it had a light blue tint to it. She wore a cutaway dress without sleeves. It was short in the front and long behind. The dress was a blue-green ombre effect. Seaweed clung to her calves, hanging. She usually kept her eyes closed, listening to the sounds and minds around her. When she opened her eyes, water appeared to flow through the bluish-green irises. She didn't always seem to be in the present, as if in a daze. This was probably because she was usually reading others' minds. She didn't say much, but when she did, it was almost always annoying. Occasionally, it would be useful, but mostly annoying. Her nails were naturally blue, and her skin was pale as the moon.

"Princess Currentide!" a voice shrieked a whisper behind her.

Currentide whipped around. She should've been paying better attention to her surroundings; she didn't notice her personal attendant was nearby until he had spoken. She must become better. Yes, she must practice more and more.

What is it? she asked her personal attendant, Flowon, via mind waves. *I'm busy.*

He looked around, as if someone might be watching, then looked back at Currentide. He whispered, "You know you aren't supposed to leave the castle unless it's absolutely necessary! When you're parents find out… Do you have any idea how much trouble I'll get in? I'll probably get fired!"

Flowon didn't usually speak with his mind. Currentide didn't know why. Currentide slowly cocked her head and smiled that wicked smile of hers. *Would you like me to find out how much trouble you might get in?*

Flowon pulled at his hair. "Just come with me!"

He grabbed her wrist, and they swam back to the castle. Currentide laughed internally. He was such a funny boy. The two had known each other their whole lives. Flowon had been assigned to watch Currentide at almost all times. At the very least he was supposed to know where she could be found if she needed to be contacted. Flowon was only a couple of years older than Currentide. He was like an older brother to her. At least, it was what she imagined having a brother must be like.

One of her favorite things to do was to mess with him. She found it humorous to watch him stress out. She probed his mind to find out what it was they were doing.

She's always at the base of my troubles. Why do I even stay here? I could easily leave the castle and go start a family somewhere nice. Yes, maybe I will do just that.

But what if Queen Mizu and King Mul don't accept my resignation? Will they have to find someone else to attend to Currentide? I don't think she can handle being on her own. Can anyone actually handle being around her all the time like I have? I'm not sure how many others can deal with her constant shenanigans without losing their sanity.

Sigh. *I'm stuck with this job aren't I?*

There was a hiatus in his thoughts. Currentide hadn't found out what she had originally wanted to, but it was still fun to see what others thought about things. It's hard to lie in one's thoughts. She knew that much from the way many people had blatantly lied to her face. This was one reason why she loved to read the thoughts of others. She picked up on Flowon's thoughts once again.

So I'll drop Currentide at her class, then maybe afterward, I can snatch a muffin from the kitchen!

Currentide couldn't resist an internal laugh. Flowon seemed outwardly confused, for he stopped. She quieted down quickly.

Currentide? he ventured. She made sure to block her mind from his whilst reading his. She had accomplished this much with the ability given to the Water Kingdom. *Currentide, I know you're there. Stop reading my thoughts! It's really annoying, you know.*

He glared at her the rest of the excursion to her classroom. After Flowon dropped her off, Currentide made a point to send him a very clear message through mind waves.

I hope you enjoy your muffin!

She laughed inwardly as he stormed away. Life was so much fun when one had the chance to badger people, especially when no one else knew what was going on.

Currentide's teacher made an obvious cough. She turned around and smiled cheekily.

I'm on time, right? She sent.

Her teacher simply shook her head and pointed in front of her. While feigning being upset, Currentide moved obligingly. Her teacher, Ms. Whiteside, taught the boring lesson. This was usual and Currentide was used to it, so she did what she usually did when she was bored: she keyed into Ms. Whiteside's thoughts or, at the very least, tried to key in. This was hard since her teacher had a stupendous mind block. Mind blocks were like shields. Its strength varied from person to person and was based off of how long one could hold the shield up. It made Currentide angry, so she strived to enter it during practically every lesson. Usually, she spent more time trying to look into Ms. Whiteside's thoughts than the lesson she "had to know if she ever wanted to be queen one day." This was her teacher's lame excuse for "you better pay attention because I said so."

"Currentide, why don't you ever pay attention when I teach class?" asked Ms. Whiteside.

Well, thought Currentide, knowing Ms. Whiteside was listening. *To be truthful, your lectures don't seem important, but my lack of paying attention is not in vain. As you hopefully didn't know, I've been trying to pass through the gateway of your mind. So it's not that I haven't been paying attention, it's that I've been focusing on another area I will need to know when I become queen.*

Ms. Whiteside sighed. She placed a hand on her forehead, a headache arising. This was one of the really bad ones only a princess such as Currentide could cause.

"Currentide," she said, "please use your words. You know, the ones that you actually have to use your vocal chords to produce? We'd all appreciate it if you did that more often."

Currentide pouted. She really hated talking verbally. She crossed her arms.

"Fine," she said. "Happy? I'm using words."

Her teacher sighed happily. Now they could finally get onto the lesson.

But you can't stop me from speaking with my mind all *of the time*, Currentide thought to her teacher with a smirk.

Ms. Whiteside marched out of the classroom as Flowon walked in. He sighed, muffin in hand.

"Don't tell me you've scared off another teacher, Currentide?" he said.

Currentide jerked her head away as if she was mad at Flowon.

It's the teacher's fault. They never let me have any fun.

Flowon sighed and gave in to speaking through mind waves.

You do realize you're always the one who makes them leave, right? he thought. *If you weren't so troublesome—*

Then life wouldn't be any fun, she interrupted.

With that, she swam away, leaving Flowon no other choice than to follow her. After a while, Flowon asked Currentide where they were going.

To the library, duh, she replied. *You know, Flowon, you should really try reading my thoughts once in a while. It makes life so much* easier. *You don't have to ask questions. You can simply* know. *It's a wonderful thing, really.*

You do realize if I ever tried to read your mind I'd fail miserably, right? Currentide laughed inside. It was a skill she had obtained over the years. Flowon continued. *Your barriers are tighter than anyone else's I've ever known.*

Yours can easily be like mine too. You just have to train unceasingly.

Oh yes, because I definitely have time to do that.

Currentide laughed again as they entered the library. Knowledge was her favorite thing to gain. Usually when she wasn't reading the minds of others, she was reading books. These books were special. They were all encased in bubbles so they could withstand being underwater. In order to easily read them, the readers were required to encase themselves in bubbles. These bubbles had a tube-like hole leading only to the gills on the reader. The books weren't damaged this way, and the Water people could easily read.

Currentide loved to read. Flowon was dragged into the library quite often. Sometimes he squirmed which made Currentide resort to more…drastic measures by making his mind want to go into the library. This was working on being such a time.

Why are you afraid of books so much, Flowon? she thought to him. *Are you scared I'm going to throw one at you if I get bored?*

Oh no, he replied. *If you threw a book at me, I'd wonder who you were and what you had done with Currentide. If you damaged a book, I'd be seriously concerned for your health.*

No, he continued. *I just don't understand why you spend so much time in here anyway. What if your parents had something for you to do?*

If my parents wanted me to do something, she thought, *then they'd communicate through mind waves. You don't realize how much simpler it is to do so. Speaking of communication, I need to tell my parents to get me another teacher.*

Currentide changed her manner of mind-speaking, so both of her parents may receive her message. Her parents had the best mind blocks there were. She knew she'd never be able to get pass the barriers they had put up. Luckily, the ability of the Water people allowed them to send messages to each other. That was all many were able to do. It was very handy to have.

Hey, Mom. Hey, Dad. Um…I kind of accidentally caused another teacher to leave.

She put her shield up quickly, not wishing them to become angry. They didn't do it often, but Currentide feared the day it happened. She was afraid they would somehow take away her birthright for simply having a little bit of fun.

Let's go read, she thought to Flowon.

Surely books would distract her. Yes, books were the answer to her problems. They were perfect. She decided to read about the history of her kingdom once again. Maybe this would put her back on her parents' good side. Yes, that was what she would do.

She pulled a few books off the shelves and created a bubble for herself. As usual, she read about the War.

"The War began long before the battles were actually fought. Some think the War lasted from the day the battles started, until they ended. I say they began years before all of that ever happened. Most say the War happened because the Four Kingdoms got together. Those people don't realize the kingdoms had already traded and spoken to each other since the beginning of time. Haven't they heard of the Creation story?

"All these people give me a headache. They should really just leave people who were actually there to write history.

"Anyway, I'm here to give you the actual story of the War and its start. It had nothing to do with trading or anything political. Every month, the eight leaders got together and discussed how things were going and how the next month should pan out. They stated their plans and other similar things.

"It was my job to record this every time. I had to write down almost everything they said. This was easy since I am from the Air Kingdom. Almost every other day, I worked in a printing shop with my wife. We would import parchment from the Earth Kingdom and print our own things. The castle job earned more money than the printing shop, but I refused to move my family.

"One time on an occasion such as the one described previously, Fire King Tân raised some questions.

"He asked, 'What would happen if our different peoples had children? Would they appear to belong in one kingdom? Would their powers be of one kingdom, or would they have both? Think of all of the possibilities! Say a male Water and a female Fire had children. Would they all read minds, see visions, control water, and control fire? Or would one read minds and control fire while another have visions and control water, or would they create an entire new element?

"'I say we take volunteers from each kingdom and try this out as an experiment.'

"'Absolutely not,' said the Earth Queen, Dharatī'. 'It has never been done before. I don't feel it would be wise to have the chance of deformed children. What if Water and Air had a child? How would he breathe? Where would he be accepted into society?'

"'You don't understand,' Fire Queen Aga replied. 'Tân has had a vision. It must happen, and you know it.'

"'The future can easily be rewritten.'

"A full-fledged argument rang out. I was barely able to write most of it down. I'm not even sure how much of it I understood. This happened when it was winter.

"The rage had boiled, and I could tell Fire King Tân had never let it go. It had been slowly building up over time. Eventually he had enough. The Fire Kingdom declared war on the Earth Kingdom. The Earth Kingdom didn't accept, but the Fire Kingdom attacked anyway. Somehow it became an all-out war between all four of the kingdoms, lasting years upon years. Eventually, no one knew why they were fighting anymore. They put their weapons down, declaring peace. All eight of the queens and kings agreed to stay separate, so another war would not happen again."

Thus, Currenilde began another book.

4

Fire

Laughter resounded about the room. It was undeniably Pyra, the Fire Princess. She loved to laugh, usually at others. She also attracted attention from others quite easily.

Her lips were a glowing red. Some would call it sexy. Her eyes showed that she was always excited. They glowed with a light you see in kids. They burned shades of orange and yellow with the occasional white speckle. Her hair was kept short. It spiked in several directions with side swept bangs. It was bright blond with pale orange streaks. She wore dark, tight, leather clothing. The top stretched across her arms and ended around her ribs, exposing her belly button. Pyra wore skintight pants. Her feet were charcoal black from all the ashes from after a fire was put out. She was always hyped up, ready for something new, different, and not her day-to-day life. She was easily angered, so most didn't mess with her too much for fear of what might happen to them afterward. Her nails were naturally red. She also had an orange skin tone, as if she had a bad fake tan.

Pyra was easily a dude magnet. They swarmed to her like fireflies to lanterns. They usually told really bad jokes, which she kind of liked. One of the good things for her was whenever she was finished making fun of them, she could easily get them out of her sight. She guessed being a princess did have some perks. Albeit, it didn't always work out that way.

"Ahem. Princess Pyra?"

"Hm?"

She turned to look at the voice. Her smile faded once she saw who it was. She glared at the intruder. The guys around her whispered to one another, knowing very well who man was.

"What do you want now?" she sighed.

The man crossed his arms. One eyebrow was raised.

"Need I even tell you?"

Pyra threw her head back and rolled her eyes. Teachers could be so annoying sometimes. She said nothing and walked ahead of her firemaster, Elswood. He followed behind. They both knew where they were going, so it didn't matter who led.

They walked into the castle and headed for the training area where Pyra would meet up with her parents. The four would train together, teaching each other what they could. For Pyra, it was meant to be a learning experience and nothing more. Personally, she still felt as if she was being treated like a child. She could teach them, too, if only they'd let her.

"You're late," scolded Queen Kasai, Pyra's mother.

"So?" Pyra replied, not caring.

"So," Elswood said, "you've caused all of us to wait. You've taken away our practice time. You also know it's important as a future queen to be punctual."

The princess sighed heavily. Why did being a princess have so many rules?

"Fine," she said, hands on hips. "We can start practicing. Let's not waste any more 'precious time.' I'm waiting. Are we starting soon? What happened to your speech about—"

Pyra was hit with a fireball by her father. She gave him a look and fired back. He created a firm shield, causing the fireball Pyra threw to ricochet and hit her mother instead.

Kasai, having not seen from where the fireball came, threw fire at all three of her opponents. It was now every man or woman for himself or herself. Shots fired from everyone almost constantly.

Practice did not usually go like this. Usually, Hwajae, Kasai, and Elswood taught each other and Pyra something new he or she had discovered or created. Hours later, they finally declared peace.

"I can't take it anymore," Hwajae said. "I think I might be getting too old for this."

"Yes," agreed Kasai.

They were all breathing heavily save Elswood.

"I could've…kept…going…" Prya said in between breaths. "I can…do this…forever…"

Elswood's arms were crossed.

"I'm sure you could have," he said sarcastically with a roll of the eyes. "You all need more training if that little fight wore you out."

All three of the royalty looked at Elswood, annoyed. After their breath was caught up, Pyra's parents left to rule the kingdom, while Elswood said he had "business to attend to." Pyra simply rolled her eyes and went to her room to take a nap.

Hours later, she awoke to being pulled off of her fire bed by a little girl. Her face smacked against the hot floor. She moaned, annoyed that she was awoken from her rest.

"Pyra, wake up!" said the little girl's voice.

The girl was pulling Pyra's arms, trying to get her to stand up. Frankly, it was annoying Pyra greatly. Hadn't anyone ever heard of the wonderful thing called napping?

She looked to see who was causing her all of this trouble. This was a mistake Pyra refused to make again.

"You're awake!" the girl squealed. She ran about the room, arms straight out as if she was trying to fly. "Now we can go play games together and have fun and Pyra could be nice for once, and ooh! Maybe we could…"

The girl continued to rattle off nonsense. Pyra moaned as she sat up. She saw her cousin on her father's side, Helen.

"Helen," she said. "What in the world are you doing here? How did you even get in? I sealed my room off."

"Oh, that's an easy question!" she replied, still running around the room. "Helen needed to get in, so Helen told a nice person she needed to get in, so the nice lady let Helen inside."

"But why are you here? Isn't it Damian's turn to babysit you today? And why are you speaking in third person again? Has your mom taught you nothing?"

"Oh, didn't Mommy tell you?" Helen answered, ignoring the last two questions. "Damian got sent off into the military, so now Helen gets to be babysat by Princess Pyra all the time!"

This was not good. Pyra enjoyed her life where she could do nothing all day long. Why did Damian have to go sign off to be in the military anyway? Now Pyra had to take care of this little kid all day.

"Hey, squirt," Pyra said. She proceeded to put on a fake happy face, complete with the high-pitched voice. "Do you want to play hide-and-seek?"

This was how Pyra usually got rid of Helen. Helen would hide, and Pyra would never look for her. Usually Pyra's aunt would get mad, but Pyra knew Helen would always leave the hiding place once she got hungry or had to use the bathroom. It at least gave Pyra time to relax for an hour, give or take.

"No," Helen said. "I don't want to play hide-and-seek today."

She stopped to place a hand on her hip and point a finger accusingly.

"You never find me anyway! I think you just want to get rid of me."

"I don't find you because you're so good at hiding."

Helen's finger fell a little. "It is true Helen is a good hider," she said. "But I still don't believe you!"

"Okay," said Pyra, lying back on her bed. "How about we play naptime?"

"I'm not tired!" Helen nearly screamed.

Pyra slapped her hands to her ears. "Kid, quiet down, will ya? Do you want the whole castle to hear you?"

Sheesh, Pyra thought. *And my parents said I was a brat.*

"Fine," she said, giving in to Helen. "What do you want to do?"

Helen's eyes shone with delight. "I wanna play elements!"

Pyra smiled evilly. This could be interesting.

"Okay," Pyra said with a wave of her hand. "I'll be fire and—"

"No!" Helen stomped her foot. "Helen picks who gets which element!"

Pyra put her hands up in defeat. "All right, all right. You pick our elements. Can you just do it quieter and not referring to yourself as a narrator?"

Satisfied, Helen grabbed Pyra's wrist and ran. This caught Pyra off-guard. Pyra was forced to awkwardly walk bent over, since she was a good deal taller than Helen. Pyra didn't have to ask where they were going since they soon arrived at one of the many balconies of the castle.

"Okay," said Helen. "I'll be Water, and Pyra can be Air."

Pyra rolled her eyes. Whatever. Helen grabbed her neck.

"Oh no!" she said. "I can't breathe! This fire from this kingdom is too hot for my gills! I'm going to dddddiiiiiiii-iieeeeeeeeeee…"

She drew out the last word, causing Pyra to roll her eyes.

Oh, brother, she thought. *I seriously have to deal with this almost every day? How will I even survive?*

She was looking away, searching for something better to do with her time when it happened. Helen was leaning backward over the balcony, acting like she was about to fall off when she lost her balance and actually fell off. Pyra turned her head at the absence of Helen's annoying voice. It was unusual for Helen to be silent.

This was when she noticed Helen wasn't there. Getting worried she would be held responsible for Helen's death, had she happen to die, Pyra surged over to the balcony and looked down. Far below her, she saw the outline of Helen's body. It was a long drop, and Pyra guessed she still had time to rescue Helen.

She dived over the balcony. She sent strong flames sparking behind her for an extra boost. Pyra needed to reach Helen before Helen hit the ground. She knew Helen was too young to be able to know how to save her own sorry butt. Soon enough, she was at Helen's side. She righted herself and stopped the flames.

To her surprise, Helen was laughing.

"Pyra! Pyra!" she squealed. "Look! We're from the Air Kingdom!"

Pyra seriously considered dropping Helen. She realized, however, it would be more troublesome to come up with an excuse of how she didn't kill Helen and knew nothing about it.

"You're lucky I'm lazy, kid," she said to Helen.

Helen simply cocked her head in confusion. Pyra moaned and rescued Helen, taking her to back inside the castle.

"Where are we going, Pyra?" Helen asked.

"Somewhere I won't have to deal with you," she growled.

"Okay! Do you think afterward we play elements again?"

"Nope."

"Aw, but, Pyra—"

"Nope."

Pyra tried to find the nursery, but the directions were too confusing. She asked Helen if she knew which resulted in more of Helen's ramblings. Wanting to pull out her hair very much, Pyra finally just fell down in a hallway.

"Pyra?" asked Helen. "Pyra are you sleeping?"

"Pyra is not here right now," she said in an annoyed voice. "If you would like to send her a message, please wait."

Helen patiently waited for a whole two minutes.

"Pyra, wake up!"

Helen proceeded to slap Pyra's face. Pyra simply found this to be a nuisance, which could be dealt with easily. Eventually, Helen got bored enough to sit next to Pyra and draw pictures in the ash floor with her finger. Her stomach finally growled.

"Pyra?" she said. "I'm hungry."

Pyra shot up, finally knowing where to get rid of Helen. She picked up Helen and placed Helen on her shoulders. Helen laughed in delight. Pyra ran into the kitchen.

Once in there, she set Helen down on a counter.

"What are you doing?" asked the head chef feverishly. She was obviously not a local. "You put dirty child on my countertop! I should smack your hand!"

She slapped the spatula in hand on the counter, causing Pyra to flinch.

"Well," Pyra said quickly, "she's your problem now. Be careful, she's prone to fall out of balconies. You have no say in this because I order you as the princess to watch over her."

The chef tried to protest but appeared unable to find the right words. Pyra left and, having nothing better to do, wandered around the castle.

5

Kidnappings

Mr. Sruli was watching over Petunia.

"Excuse me?" said a nurse. "I don't know your relation with that girl, but visiting hours are closed."

"Oh," he said. "I'm sorry. I was there when the accident happened and wanted to make sure she was in good hands before I left. She was one of my better students."

The nurse smiled.

"Don't worry, we have everything under control."

Mr. Sruli stood up, gave a curt nod, and left. After the nurse was positive Mr. Sruli and everyone else were out of sight, the nurse took Petunia out of the hospital bed. The nurse carried Petunia out the back through secluded hallways.

When the nurse was at the vehicle, the nurse tied up Petunia's hands and feet and placed her in a bag. The nurse drove off, kicking up dust.

"Hey, Currentide," Flowon said. "Put the books up, your maid will kill me if you get to bed late again. Don't make her yell at me again."

Currentide popped her bubble.

Okie-doke, she thought to him. *I'll let you have the freedom of not being yelled at tonight.*

She went to the bookcases and shelved her books.

"Excuse me," said a voice. "Could you help me find this book?"

As she turned to the person, everything went black. She hadn't even sensed the perpetrator's presence. The person, seeing little means of escape, decided to take advantage of Flowon.

"Sir?" the person said, approaching Flowon and carrying Currentide on its back. "This girl fainted or something. I was just trying to ask her about a book…"

"What!" exclaimed Flowon. "We need to get her to a doctor immediately! Follow me!"

The person followed Flowon until the entrance to the castle was visible. The person decided to take leave and swam away. Flowon didn't notice.

The person swam far away from the castle, thinking Currentide was heavier than she looked. The person shoved Currentide into the small room of the submarine. Water escaped, and the person could breathe easily once again. The girl on the other hand…

After taking the gear off, the perpetrator tied her feet and hands together then put her in a bag. The person had brought a tub onto the vehicle and filled it with water. The perpetrator proceeded to put the girl in it and then drove away, propellers spinning furiously.

A shadowy figure snuck into the bedroom. It crept around, careful to make as little sound as possible. Of course, that was pretty easy to accomplish in the clouds. The figure took off the covers and tied up the Cirrus's hands and feet.

It picked her up then carried her away. The figure was careful when carrying Princess Stratus around the castle. If anyone knew what it was doing, the entire cover would be blown.

After exiting the castle, the figure boarded the plane. It put her in a bag then sat itself in the cockpit and flew the vehicle away. The figure hoped none of the princesses awoke during any of the traveling. It would be too costly. The figure drove slowly solely for this reason.

Pyra was beginning to think she was lost in the castle. She couldn't always find her way around because her parents were constantly renovating it. How dark was it outside anyway? She should probably be heading to bed. A yawn came upon her. Yup, it was time to hit the fire.

After taking a few steps, an arm shot out for her throat. She ducked and kicked the darkness, hoping to hit the body that was surely in there. Something made a noise, and she could only hope it was her opponent.

She made a small fireball in her hand and approached her attacker.

"Now," she said. "Let's see who would attack young girls at night, shall we?"

Someone pulled her ankles, causing Pyra to fall. She felt something cold and hard hit her head. A shiver was sent throughout her entire body. Cold did not feel good, she found out before going into nothingness.

The partners in crime locked eyes and nodded. They had previously spoken about their jobs, albeit there was a complaint causing one of them to receive a blow to the head. There weren't arguments afterward. Now they did their tasks with fast silence.

Now that the princess was tied and bagged, the two left the castle and entered their vehicle. They drove away from the Fire Kingdom, hoping to not get burned more than necessary.

6

Awakening

The room was plain, gray, harsh. It had a simple design of four walls, a bed in each corner with a bedside table next to each one, a rusty mirror, a dresser, a door, and strange rectangular prisms in the corners. There were no windows, but there was a strange object on the ceiling, which emitted a weird light. When one entered the room, Fire's bed was closest on the right. Water's was in the right far corner. In between the two was the mirror. On the left, Air's bed was first, followed by the dresser, and Earth's bed was in the back corner. The princesses weren't accustomed to sleeping on odd things called mattresses that lay upon tungsten bed frames.

The first experiences they felt were the sensation of cold, lack of water, death, and shortness of breath. All four of the princesses awoke on the same day in the same room.

Easily enough, Earth was the first to awake; those from the Earth Kingdom were early risers. She looked at her surroundings. Where was she? Who were these other girls? She hoped they were kind and nice. They didn't look like they were from her kingdom.

She struggled to remember the last thing to happen to her. She couldn't bring it to mind. Her feet touched the floor for a millisecond. It was not like the ones she had back in the castle. It was hard, so hard.

She looked over to see one of the girls convulsing in her sleep. The want to help her overcame Earth. She moved swiftly across the harsh floor to a girl with long hair. Earth tentatively shook her awake.

"Um, excuse me?" she said. The girl looked at her with wide eyes. "You were—"

The girl gasped then quickly closed her mouth. Earth was very confused.

"Is there something I can do for you?"

"W…"

Earth cocked her head, trying to make sense of the situation.

"Wa… wat-t…"

Earth thought a little.

"Water! Is that what you need?"

The girl nodded feverishly. Earth looked around the room. There wasn't anything in the way of water. Her eyes locked onto the dresser. She moved over to it for closer inspection. It felt like wood, but…it didn't seem to have life in it at all. It seemed like a case containing nothing. Could she still make life out of it to help?

Earth tried with all her might to make plants from it. Plants had water in them; maybe she could help somehow in this way. She made five of the most water-filled plants she knew of grow from the dead wood. Even though there wasn't any more life in it, her powers still allowed Earth to create new life. It was a strange thing to Earth, for there wasn't such a thing in the Earth Kingdom as a plant without life.

She brought the plants over to the girl, saying, "Here."

Then a peculiar thing happened. The girl, Water, extracted water from the plants. She grouped it all together and placed in on her gills. Earth had failed to notice them earlier.

Earth thought she had heard a sound similar to "th." She figured Water must have stuttered for almost instantaneously, Water quickly said, "Thank you very much."

Earth smiled.

"Oh, you're welcome!" she replied with a small laugh. In the Earth Kingdom, laughter was a sign of true happiness. "Always happy to help!"

Water sat up and pulled her legs in close. She latched her hands around them. Another girl with long hair, hers being gray, awoke.

"Who are you?" she immediately asked. "Why are you here? Where am I? It feels weird in here. The air is…"

She shook her head.

"No," she continued. "This isn't air…"

"Is there a way I can help you?" Earth asked. "I don't think I can answer most of your questions, but I'd be happy to be your friend, dearest acquaintance."

Air gave Earth a funny look.

"Of course," said Earth. "That's only if you want to."

"Oh, I wasn't trying to give off that impression. It's just you're so far below me I'm not sure if we should even be talking. I've spoken with commoners before, but I'm not sure how I'm supposed to deal with a…a *foreigner*."

Earth was still smiling.

"It's all right," she said. "I don't mind."

A snore made Earth jump. All three girls looked at the one still sleeping.

"Should we—" started Earth when the sleeping girl rolled out of her bed and onto the floor.

Internally, Water was laughing. She knew what just happened. The others perceived it to be normal until the remaining female jumped up and onto the bed.

"WHAT IN THE WORLD WAS THAT?!" she yelled.

Air laughed; Earth became concerned. The remaining girl, Fire, dusted herself off.

"As if you wouldn't have reacted had the same thing happened to you."

Air laughed harder, now clutching her sides. Fire wrapped her blanket around her body tightly.

"Does anyone else think it's cold in here?"

Everyone became solemn. They all didn't feel like they should be here; something felt wrong. It was nothing like home. Where was home? How far was it? Would they ever return?

The four sat in silence, all thinking about their kingdoms. Home. It was like they knew things but couldn't quite remember everything. They knew who they were, Earth, Water, Air, Fire; what their kingdom was like; and how to use their different powers and abilities but couldn't quite place faces with names. They couldn't remember their own names, only what elements they were.

The door opened.

All four heads turned toward it. A woman in dark clothes and fuzzy, white, toeless feet entered. She was careful to keep her hand on the doorknob. She wore frames over her eyes with something dark inside. They could not see what color her eyes were nor if she indicated anything through them. Her red hair was kept in a high ponytail. Her nails and lips were the same color as her skin. She also held a strange, flat object in her hand, but it looked to be more stable than parchment. She was...odd.

"You four need to come with me," she said.

The girls struggled to choose whether or not to cling to each other. They weren't from the same kingdoms, but they might be the closest thing to home they'd ever get again.

They were taken across the cold floor. It wasn't too far a walk; however, every cold step felt like a century to Pyra and Petunia. The woman lifted a curtain and motioned for them to step through. They did so tentatively.

There was a light behind a shadowy figure. All but Fire and Air felt blinded.

"Hello," he said.

Fire crossed her arms, already annoyed. She just wanted to get out of there as fast as possible. She began tapping her foot impatiently.

"And welcome," he finished, trying to be dramatic.

Fire took a deep breath. He better hurry it up…

"So…how are you?"

She could contain herself no longer. Her eyes shone with a growing hatred. Fire began to form on her hands and feet.

"You want to know how I *am?* Do you *seriously* want to know? Because I'll tell you!"

"Um, no, it's a rhetor—"

"I'm fine! Just fine! I was just kidnapped from my home and placed in a frozen room! And that blue chick looks like she's hyperventilating, which is *really* getting on my nerves."

The figure snapped and muttered saying, "I knew I forgot *something* when they got here."

"You think you're real smart, don't you? Oh, yes, everything's just *dandy!*"

"You see—" he started, but never got to finish.

"She's not the only one who has problems!" Air piped up. "Did you really expect *them*"—she gestured to the other girls—"to be good enough to room with *me?* They're really weird. And don't think you're accommodations will *ever* be good enough for a *princess*! I don't know how you people breathe, seriously."

She crossed her arms with a huff and turned her head away.

The figure was hunched forward, his head in his hands. What was he supposed to do? Was he supposed to listen or fight back? With an iron fist, he made a decision. He looked back up at them.

"Princesses!"

They all quieted down, shocked by his loud voice. "Look, you're my captives, okay? I'm the one in charge here. *I* make all the decisions."

He got up so fast his chair fell over.

He left the area, saying, "Natascha, make sure they get put back."

The woman merely nodded in response. She did as she was told, closing the door behind her. They were once again trapped. They hadn't even fought back when corralled back into their room. Earth immediately went over to the fallen flowers and picked them up. She curled up on her bed, clutching them tightly.

She had never seen that much hatred in one person before. How could whoever it was live with himself? He could never, ever be from the Earth Kingdom.

Fire became cold once again. She needed fire. Sitting on her bed, she created a small flame. Soon, her whole bed was consumed, and she felt much, much better. The others cringed away at the fire, afraid they were staring death in the face. Earth was glad she was on the opposite side of the room, but she was also glad Fire was able to make her bed a little more like home.

Air looked at the others. Why was she paired with *them*? It made sense for her to be kidnapped, obviously since she was a princess, but them? Why, she'd rarely heard of any other princesses before. They couldn't *possibly* be princesses as well; it seemed fictitious.

Water wished for a book. How was she supposed to pass the time in here? Reading three other people's minds was only going to be interesting for only so long. She pondered on her kidnappers, making sure to keep tabs on the other three and the water on her gills. She mentally sighed. Why couldn't her kidnapper have lived underwater?

Everyone was silent as the fire crackled. What were they supposed to do now? What next? Were they supposed to sit and see what happened? Wait for someone to rescue them? Or were they supposed to fight and try to escape?

Everyone was confused. No one had ever been here before. They had a feeling their captors wouldn't tell them the ways of this place. Was it a kingdom? They all had many questions but knew it was pointless to voice them.

Earth began to cry softly. She had never imagined being this far away from home before. There was also no way she knew of to help the others. This was the greatest pain she had ever felt. For the first time in her life, she was unable to help someone else, and it made her feel without purpose.

"C-can we…" she said. "Can we recite the Creation story?"

She wanted something to hold on to. Even if a story wasn't tangible, it was a reminder of home, of where she came from. She knew the others simply must be from the other kingdoms; they had to be. If they weren't…

Earth felt the Creation story went beyond a normal story. It was the beginning of the most wonderful thing in the entire world. It was a tale of life, of everything.

The others mulled over these words. Was there harm in telling the Creation story? In this place of unfamiliar things, it seemed…strange. As if it shouldn't be there, a rebellious thing to do. Yet why shouldn't they bring something close to their hearts into the place of unfamiliarity?

It was Fire who spoke up to make the decision.

"Yes," she said.

And so, Earth started the story. The other girls pitched in details from their kingdoms or took over complete parts.

Occasionally, Water added a word or two. She mostly kept to herself.

They started at the beginning, the beginning of everything imagined.

The Creation Story

The Creator looked at what there was in the world, the light and darkness. He decided He needed four elements for the life He would later create. He created earth for the life to lie upon. He created air, for life to breathe. He created water, for the life to drink and be sustained. He created fire, so the life may be warm.

Rather than keeping all these elements together, He separated them into four sections, which He called kingdoms. In each of these sections, He created two rulers to live in and provide these elements. They were a man and a woman and didn't need the other elements in order for their own life to be sustained; this was part of the beauty in it all.

"All this land is for you," He told each pair, showing them their section. "You shall be its leaders. You are equal in supremacy, neither man nor woman is stronger or weaker."

He gave each of the kingdoms a gift of power. He allowed them all to control their element, but no more. With these powers, they created castles to live in, according to their own tastes and needs. The powers were at their greatest strength in the beginning. They lived separate lives, not knowing of the others' existences.

One day, He collected the rulers.

"Each of you has your own section to rule. You must communicate with each other and rule together. This world needs all four of you working in harmony in order to survive. You are all part of one body, and no element is more important than the other. If you need me, you know where to find me. Peace be with you."

He left, not to be seen for many more years. Finally, there was a question.

"Oh, powerful Creator," said Water. "What if we had a people to rule over? It is very lonely ruling by ourselves."

So the Creator created other beings with the same likeness as each of the rulers. The rulers had a people to rule over. It was less lonely. There were parties and good times throughout the kingdoms. Everyone was happy and worshipped the Creator. The rulers had many children. All who lived in the kingdoms were prosperous.

Until, one of the children spoke up. He was a child in the Air Kingdom; it was summer.

"Creator!" he said. "I know You love the Air Kingdom the best. You should give us a power to control the other kingdoms."

The Creator didn't respond. The child was persistent, causing this want for more to bleed into his teenage years. He gave the child the ability to remember everything that had happened to him.

"Know," the Creator said. "This is a gift."

It was a blessing and a curse; all of his worst moments were stuck in his head forever.

This story reached the ears of a child of the Water Kingdom. She heard about a man in the Air Kingdom receiving an ability from the Creator. She spoke to the Creator.

"Dearest Creator," she said. "I know You can tell the Water Kingdom is merely doing what You have required of us. I only have one request. There's someone in the Air Kingdom to whom You gave a special ability to. I wish for an ability as well."

She, too, was persistent. He gave in and gave her the ability to read others' minds.

"Know," the Creator said. "This is a gift."

She was outcasted by her peers. No one wanted to be friends with someone who knew all of one's secrets.

A person from the Fire Kingdom heard about abilities given to people her age and asked the Creator a question as well.

"Creator," she said. "Why is it You give abilities to people of the Air and Water Kingdoms? Are You not watching the Fire Kingdom? We are the least prosperous of all. Surely, we deserve something too!"

The Creator gave this young adult an ability as well, knowing she, too, would be persistent. He gave her the ability to see the future at only select times. The timing was never the same.

"Know," the Creator said. "This is a gift."

She hid from society, not wanting others to see her receive a vision.

Many years passed. The three with both abilities and powers were elders now. The Earth Kingdom had yet to have a person with an ability. None of them thought the Earth Kingdom would ever receive one. Why should they ask something of the Creator who was all-powerful and all-controlling? They thought if He wanted someone to have an ability, it was His choice to give it.

All thought this way except for one.

He was the same age as the others. Now, in his old age, he was slowly dying. He lay in bed most of the time. One day, he pondered upon these others who had abilities. He, too, began to question the Creator.

"Almighty Creator," he said. "You know I have been Your faithful servant. I simply wonder why in the other kingdoms, there is talk of people who have abilities You gave them. Is this true? It is said in the beginning, You talked of equality many times. Where has that equality gone, I wonder?

"I know I am old in age and shouldn't have even asked these questions, but why have you not given the Earth Kingdom an ability? I apologize for my ignorance, oh, Powerful One."

"My son," he said. The elder was speechless. The Creator was talking to *him*! He had no words for the Creator. "It is because your kingdom has not asked me that you don't have an ability. Now, I give you the greatest of the gifts I have given. I give you the gift of wisdom.

"What you have spoken is true. I have not upheld My idea of equality, because I was waiting to give you your ability of wisdom."

He said the next words to everyone in all of the kingdoms.

"I now give these abilities that I have given to the four people, one from each kingdom, to everyone in their respectable kingdoms. In addition to your power to control your element, you have the respectable ability as well.

"Air, you have the ability to remember everything. You will never forget. Water, you can read the minds of those around you. Be patient with one another. Fire, you have the ability to see the future. You won't know when it will come next. Earth, you have the greatest ability of all. You have a great wisdom.

"I do this in the hope you can become closer. Air sees the past, Water reads the present, Fire sees the future, and Earth reads wisdom in decisions. These four abilities are necessary for oncoming events. You must work together in order to survive anything.

"I must go now. You'll still be able to make contact. Peace be with you all."

With that, the Creator left. Not as many bothered Him after the Last Meeting, as it came to be known as later on. The people of the kingdoms heard little of Him as time went on. They all remembered Him and remained worshipping Him.

The people found it easy to work together. The Creator had thought everything out so perfectly, since He knew what was to happen. It was an easy puzzle, where the pieces fell into place without a whole lot of thought or work needing to be done. The kingdoms lived in harmony for years to come.

8

Exploring

There was a knock at the door. The woman named Natascha walked inside, carrying trays of food. The food didn't exactly look appetizing; it appeared nothing like what they had at home.

"I brought—"

Seeing Fire's bed on fire, she stopped.

"Is there a reason your bed is on fire?" she asked.

Fire shrugged.

"I was cold," she said. "If you want me to put it out and allow myself to die, that's all right. It's fine by me."

"No, no. I was just curious. Just don't get anything else on fire, okay? Anyway, I made you each some food pertaining to your kingdom." Natascha walked to each as she handed the meal over. "Princess Pyra, I brought you some spicy enchiladas. Princess Cirrus or Princess Stratus, I brought you some angel food cake. Princess Currentide,

I brought you fish. Princess Petunia, I brought you a salad. Enjoy."

Currentide was disgusted; how dare they think someone from the Water Kingdom ever eat fish! They were vegetarians; it was hard to kill anything when one knew all the thoughts the creature had. It was like experiencing the death yourself.

Petunia attempted to eat her food since her captor was being hospitable, and it would be rude to ignore the food she was given. She couldn't get past a couple bites before apologizing to the plants. She settled to making a doll out of the plants. It reminded her of home.

Natascha left, and the four girls stared at their food. They weren't required to eat. Food was simply a delicacy, merely a form of entertainment. Food was meant to taste good, and that was all there was to it. It was about presentation and the flavors. Eating for sustainment was unnecessary. This food in particular didn't look like an exciting meal, so they all dismissed it.

"I miss home," said the Air princess.

"Hey," Pyra said, "why did she call you by two names?"

"Oh!" A smile played upon Cirrus's lips. "I had a twin as a young child. We were identical, and she's not here anymore. For all of my life, I've been called by both names since no one could figure out which one was which."

"So why don't you just let people know which name is yours? Wouldn't that be easier for everyone? I think I would have given up after a week."

Pyra stared through closed eyelids at the ceiling.

"That's the fun part," Stratus said. "No one knows except for me, and I'm certainly not telling you three."

This way no one will ever forget her, she added in her head.

Currentide knew, though, which twin she was. This was because she heard the Air Kingdom's princess's thoughts about her twin. She decided she would keep all their secrets until the time was right to reveal them.

"Well, I'll just call you Stratus, so I don't get confused," Pyra said.

"I suppose I'll call you Cirrus," said Petunia. "It's a gorgeous name."

"So who's up for a game to pass the time?"

"Ooh, we could play Plant Pets!" The others simply stared at her. "Or if you don't want to…"

"How about we play Strikers instead?" suggested Stratus. No one knew what that was either.

"Do you know how to play Conquer?" Pyra asked. They shook their heads and looked at Currentide. "Well, missy. You haven't said much. Why don't you suggest a game to play? Because if we don't play a game, I'm going to take a nap."

Currentide smiled.

"Don't worry," she said. "I'm already playing a game."

The other three gave her confused looks.

"How do we play?" Petunia asked.

"You've already been playing," said Currentide.

She laughed internally at them, outwardly looking completely serious. Maybe this would be more fun than she originally thought it would be. The others simply looked at each other. What in the world was she talking about? Confused, Pyra fell asleep, leaving Cirrus and Petunia alone. They obviously weren't getting anywhere with Currentide.

"What was it like in the Air Kingdom?" Petunia asked, knowing people loved to talk about themselves. She'd heard about the Air people changing their attitude with the seasons. If Petunia had her facts right, it was the season to be selfish and conceited.

"Well," said Stratus, "it's wonderful, obviously, since it's the best of all four of the kingdoms. The atmosphere is… different than wherever we're at now. It's thicker, making it harder for me to breathe. I feel like there's too much air down here. That's probably because it isn't air, but whatever. Rather than whatever this hard structure is, our buildings are made from clouds."

"Has anyone ever fallen through?" Petunia interrupted. She knew it was rude, but worry overcame her kindness for others.

"That's a ludicrous idea! Of course no one's ever fallen through! That's like asking if you fell into the ground! Besides, even if we did fall through, we'd just enter again by using air."

"Actually there are places where people have fallen into the ground. They're called sinkholes. Don't you think the Creator had a lot of fun when He made the kingdoms?"

Without a better comeback, Cirrus said, "Well, I'm still smarter than you!"

"I don't want to hurt your feelings, but the Creator made us all equal. The length of our intelligence seems to currently reach the edge of our pertaining kingdom lines."

Stratus blinked. *What in the world did this girl just say?* she wondered.

"Oh yeah?" She couldn't be beat by anyone else ever again. It would be so humiliating. "Well, I bet I could beat you at racing the wind."

"I have no doubt you could."

Cirrus was taken aback. She wasn't use to this humbling aspect of the Earth Kingdom. She wanted retorts and comebacks. This girl wasn't giving them to her. Petunia was calm as well, which didn't help Stratus's side of things. Cirrus turned away, not wanting to deal with Petunia and her calmness any longer.

Petunia was once again alone. Currentide was awake, but she didn't really say much. Stratus didn't want to talk with her anymore, and Pyra was sleeping. She didn't want to disturb anyone, and she didn't appear to be a whole lot of help to anyone. She curled up into a ball and thought of the festivals back home.

Everyone always had a good time at the festivals. They were full of merriment and joy. Everyone would sing and dance. The food was marvelous. There was almost incessant eating. It was a happy time in the kingdom.

Out of boredom, Cirrus stood up and walked the two steps to the door. To her surprise, it was unlocked. She looked back at Currentide and Petunia then walked outside, closing the door. Petunia flustered.

"Should we go with her?" she asked feverishly. "I don't think she should be alone. Who shall go? I do not think any of this is at all wise."

While Petunia was talking Currentide was acting. Currentide walked over to the door and followed Stratus. Petunia became worried as she sat, hoping they would come back all right. She would have gone with them but knew she couldn't leave Pyra by herself in case something bad did happen.

Cirrus simply stood for a moment, looking at her surroundings. If she ever planned on escaping, she needed to remember what she could. Remembering was the easy part; the hard part was formulating a plan. The lighting was dim, coming from the outside just as she expected. Currentide could see easily for she was accustomed to little light.

Stratus began to walk around, Currentide quietly following behind. Cirrus didn't know she was here yet.

Everything around them was old and worn down. This was peculiar, for buildings in the kingdoms never grew old.

People were always living in them, and if anything was no longer needed, the supplies were used elsewhere, or the building otherwise changed into another.

Stratus closed her eyes and remembered when they were taken out that morning. The lighting had changed slightly, but the room was the same. She looked around her now, at the tables in front of her. They were there earlier in the same formation. She noted they were untouched with boxes that said GNIGAKCAP on the side. *What a strange language*, she thought. The writing at home looked nothing like this.

She walked down one of the rows. Currentide followed silently behind.

Cirrus looked toward where their captor sat earlier. She saw the equipment she assumed was used to make such a bright light but understood none of it. At least one mystery was probably solved. She found a staircase closely behind it and began her descent.

Currentide tried her hardest to be in step with Stratus so she wouldn't be heard. She concentrated too much, which made her water splat to the ground. Hurriedly she stopped, raised the water back up to her gills, and continued on. Having not walked stairs most of her life, Currentide found out soon enough too little concentration resulted in falling.

Thus, Currentide fell onto Stratus, and they both tumbled down.

"Who goes there?" Cirrus exclaimed.

Currentide sighed, knowing her cover was blown. The two disentangled themselves from each other and stood up. Once Stratus realized it was Currentide, she was fine.

"Oh," she said. "It's you."

Well, that's a lovely name, Currentide thought. *Thanks so much for giving me such a wonderful title. I really appreciate it.*

"So," Cirrus said, "what brings you here?"

Currentide shook her head in despair. How would she ever survive?

"Anyway," she continued, "I'm just gonna keep exploring, I guess…"

Stratus continued walking around and taking in the sights, remembering them; Currentide followed once again. She quickly touched mind base with the other two in the room. Petunia wasn't dying of concern yet, and Pyra was still sleeping. Currentide had never really tested if she could read dreams or not. She decided to try it out another time. She should currently focus on the exploration.

Cirrus looked and walked. They were in a small hallway and walked single file. There were a few doors on their left. Each one had a different plate with a different word. Stratus knew she must remember them all. There was a total of six doors with seven words thus far. They entered none of the doors.

"Currentide." Currentide looked at Stratus. Cirrus had stopped for a moment to talk. "After we finish looking around this floor, why don't we head back to the room?"

Currentide nodded, and the two continued down the hallway. Straight ahead was another staircase; to their left, there were more doors. The briskly walked past, merely glancing at the plates. After getting to the end, they turned right around to walk back to their room of confinement.

They made the trek down the hallways, up the staircase, through the rows, and to the doors. Stratus turned the knob.

It didn't open.

She tried again, this time with more force. She thought maybe if she banged on the door the others would open it.

No one came to their rescue. The door remained closed. The girls were locked outside.

9

Pain

"Did you lock it back up?" he asked.

"Of course, why wouldn't I?" she retorted.

"Well, considering you didn't prior to this conversation..."

"Oh, you hush!"

She looked away; she did not want to deal with him right now, but they were in this together.

"What do you plan on doing with them?" she asked.

The silence hung in the air like an elephant in the room. It was like that for many minutes. They were both caught up in their thoughts. She wondered what his plan was. She had come up with many different ideas. Were they to become slaves? No, they could easily overcome him with their powers and abilities. Would he sell them? No, he wasn't that cruel. Was he? She didn't think he dealt in that kind of stuff, but then again she'd only known him for a few months.

"I don't know," he said. "I'm sure we'll figure something out when the time is right. As long as we stick to The Plan everything will be fine."

He surely hoped so, anyway. To be truthful, he wasn't entirely sure of The Plan. He knew their basic outline; he was the one to come up with it: kidnap the princesses, teach them to assimilate into society, and take the princesses to his leader. That was the first part. Sometimes, however, he wasn't sure if he wanted to go through with it all. He knew it was necessary, but to be honest, he didn't really like what they were doing. He didn't want to tell Natascha that, though.

She relaxed once he reminded her of The Plan. Yes, The Plan. Everything would go smoothly if they followed it. That's all she needed in order to be at peace again.

Hwajae was furious. How could they do something like this? It was an outrage! Kasai was equally angry. And to think she was considering trading with them! Not anymore. If they were to think something like this was to be funny, well, they were wrong.

Other and mutual feelings spread throughout the kingdoms about their missing daughters. The Fire Kingdom immediately accused the other kingdoms of such a catastrophe. The Earth Kingdom was stricken the Fire Kingdom would think such a thing and tried to figure out what the wisest choice would be. If they met, would another war start? The Air Kingdom was surprised the other princesses were missing as well. They struggled to remember the last events before they found out their daughter was missing. Nothing appeared out of the ordinary. The Water Kingdom watched the other kings' and queens' minds very closely. They wondered if the Fire Kingdom was right in accusing. Did one of the other leaders have their daughter?

It was very chaotic in the kingdoms outside the castle walls as well. The queens and kings had not told their people, but wandering maids tend to overhear things they shouldn't and gossip about it later.

All the kingdoms were falling apart. Without leaders to control and rule the people, the people didn't know what to do. If they hadn't found out, life would have gone as usual for them. Nothing would have changed.

Except they do know.

Petunia was pacing about the small room. *They've been gone for a while now.* She thought. *Should they be back now? Yes, they really should. Where could they be?*

Pyra yawned very loudly. Petunia was broken from her trance momentarily. Pyra looked around the room through half-closed eyelids.

"Where are the other two?" she asked sleepily.

"They went out a while ago," Petunia explained. "I'm starting to worry. They haven't come back yet."

Pyra raised an eyebrow. "Don't you, worry easily, or something?"

Petunia laughed quietly at herself. She guessed she did worry too much sometimes.

There was a banging at the door, and they flinched. They stared at it as the banging continued. Who could that be at this hour? If it was a captor, surely she would simply come in. The same went for Stratus and Currentide. Petunia looked over at Pyra. What was Pyra thinking they should do? Petunia had the sudden feeling whoever outside was friendly.

"Um, Pyra?" Petunia tentatively asked. "I think the people or person outside is friendly."

Pyra gave her a look that said "Are you serious? You dummy." She shook her head.

"No," she said. "Absolutely not. We are not opening the door for whoever it is outside."

Petunia's face fell, but she was determined. "We can't let them just stand out there! I'm opening the door!"

She walked a couple of steps and grabbed the doorknob, ready to yank it open, when Pyra threw fire at Petunia. Fire and earth don't mix, so Petunia wasn't ready for such an attack. She lay on the floor, clutching her body. She'd never been attacked before and was hurt both physically and emotionally. However, she knew she had to forgive Pyra in order for a chance at a friendship to last.

"I forgive you, Pyra," she said with a weak smile. "It's all right if you want to attack me. I'll be fine."

It was not on Pyra's agenda to apologize. It was Petunia's fault if she couldn't handle such an attack. Pyra hadn't even hit her that hard. Although, she did wonder who was outside making such a loud noise. It stopped abruptly. She walked over to the door and made a small peephole with fire through the door. She didn't have much of a chance to look in it as her eye felt blasted by wind. Pyra clutched her right eye and leaned back.

She tried to look with her left eye, but everything happening was confusing. She heard a click and watched the door open itself. She took a step back and hit her bed, causing her to tumble atop it.

Pyra was prepared to attack. Her eye was starting to feel better. She could take on whoever it was.

Two people walked in. Fire was in Pyra's hand, ready to throw. She almost did except someone stopped her.

"No!" yelled Petunia. "You can't attack them. It's Cirrus and Currentide!"

Pyra's hand fell, realizing it was their fellow captives. She crossed her arms and diminished the fire.

"Oh, you're back."

"Is there a problem with that?" Stratus challenged. Her hands were on her hips. Currentide closed the door, and

Petunia stood up, not wanting the others to worry about her. Her arms were slightly burned, but they should heal quickly. All of the elemental people healed fast.

"I just thought if someone was going to leave the room, she might as well escape while she can," Pyra said. "Anyone else would have thought of *that*."

Cirrus's hands were in fists now. "You could've left whenever you wanted to!"

"Oh, please enlighten me."

"Uh, you obviously could have burned the door down whenever you wanted to."

"Do you realize how obvious that would be? Besides, I can do it anytime I want to."

Stratus crossed her arms as well. "I could say the same for myself."

"Please stop fighting," Petunia said gently. "Maybe we're not supposed to leave, maybe all this has a greater purpose to it. I'm not entirely sure, but I feel like we shouldn't try to escape."

Pyra gave her a look. "Really? That's what you think? You are *so* dumb."

Petunia was hurt and went over to her bed. Cirrus sighed and gazed at the door. She could go memorize the rooms and the first floor… She wondered if their captors were watching them. Would they know if she left again?

As she pondered upon this, Pyra wondered why none of them had truly attempted to escape. Although they didn't know where their captors lay, they could easily have tried to get out. Was it because they believed the door to be locked? If someone always remained in the room, couldn't they get back in? She thought they should test it.

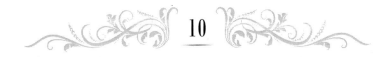

10

Obstacle Course of Fire

After "eating" and sleeping the night before, the girls woke up early the next morning to Natascha shoving more plates of food in their faces.

"Wake up!" she commanded.

The girls slowly awoke. They weren't used to people yelling at them in the morning, nor having food shoved in their faces.

"What do you want?" moaned Pyra, pushing the plate away.

Natascha crossed her arms, the flat object still in hand. "Everyone get up and follow me!"

No one ate the food.

Stratus leaned over to Currentide and whispered, "Are we going to do this every morning?"

As usual, Currentide made no response.

The group remained on the same floor. The lights were on again, and the figure was in the chair as well. Cirrus was more satisfied this time, knowing what her surroundings were like and having seen what might cause such brightness.

"Welcome!" the figure said again. "Did you enjoy your first day?"

No one replied. Petunia was still a little frightened, and the others had no desire to speak with him.

"Personally, I was hoping for more of a response, but whatever." There was silence. "Anyway, the second day has commenced, and I assure you, today will be…different. You'll find out soon enough. Just wait and see."

"I feel like all we're doing is waiting," muttered Pyra.

"What was that?" barked Natascha.

Pyra raised her eyebrows innocently as if to say, *Oh, you're talking to me?*

The figure continued to talk.

"Moving on, you may or may not have noticed the wristbands."

Currentide and Cirrus had noticed the wristbands. They knew something felt different or heavier but weren't quite sure what the object on their wrists were called. Petunia thought something was odd but didn't see the wristband until now. She made no move to try and cover up looking at it. Pyra nonchalantly looked down at her wrist. How had she missed this object called wristband?

"Today we're going to have an obstacle course. It will be done individually. You are also not allowed to use your powers during this course."

"And what's going to stop us?" Pyra challenged.

"Those wristbands will shock you immediately if you so much as attempt to use your powers."

"If these 'wristbands' are supposed to shock us, then why aren't I being shocked right now?" ventured Currentide. They all looked at her who was staying alive by using her powers.

"With the exception of Princess Currentide and her gills."

"That's not fair!" Stratus exclaimed. "If she can use her powers, then why can't we?"

The figure pinched the bridge of his nose. The girls knew his hand was on his face but not what he was doing. He sighed and continued on.

"Princess Currentide cannot breathe otherwise. We need all four of you alive."

"So if I commit suicide, your plan will be foiled?" questioned Pyra.

The figure didn't answer her question and merely replied with, "Princess Pyra, you are up first. Natascha, take the others back into the room."

The figure and Pyra stood in silence. Pyra, making sure Natascha wasn't looking, attempted to roundhouse kick her male captor. He ducked as she came back with a punch.

Pyra's arm was held back by Natascha who had returned. Pyra elbowed Natascha with her free arm. Natascha grabbed that arm also and pulled both of Pyra's arms behind Pyra's back.

The male captor stood up and blindfolded Pyra while Natascha tied Pyra's wrists together.

"Should we knock her out?" he asked.

Natascha nodded. "It will be easier to take her that way."

They knocked her out and carried her down the stairs.

Pyra awoke to darkness, for the blindfold was still on her. She felt like she was moving, but she wasn't sure since she also felt still at the same time. After a while, she felt a lurch. She knew she must have been in a vehicle, but she had never encountered such a…thing before.

She was dragged out of the vehicle and forced up on her feet. She was taken a ways from the vehicle. It would be out of her sight now. Her blindfold was taken off, and her hands were untied. She looked about herself. The obstacle course looked easy enough. One of her captors took out a small object with a trigger and thin barrel. He pulled the trigger and another button at the same time, causing a small flame to start. Just to mess with them, Pyra extinguished the flame.

He gave Natascha the signal, and a shock erupted throughout Pyra's body.

"That's what you get for using your powers," Natascha said.

Pyra grimaced. Her other captor continued on and relit the barrel. He took the flame to the obstacle course. New flames erupted throughout the entire course.

"We will be timing you," announced Natascha. "You know the rules: no powers. If you try to escape, we'll simply recapture you. You're in unfamiliar territory whereas we know this place very well."

Pyra wanted to say Natascha was bluffing about them knowing the terrain, but she couldn't be sure. Pyra glared at her captors. How stupid did they think she was to go along with all of this?

"At your heed," a kidnapper said.

Pyra crossed her arms and raised an eyebrow. She wasn't going to do what they told her. *Rebel*, her mind commanded. *Rebel*. She agreed wholeheartedly and became even more unwilling than before to conform to the ways of her captors.

Natascha pursed her lips. "If you don't do the course, we won't give you food for the next week."

Pyra made a *tch* sound. "Yes," she said with a roll of the eyes. "Because I need food to survive."

Natascha began to die a little inside. They didn't need food? She took a sideways glance at her partner. She asked him with her eyes, *Did you know?* He didn't appear to understand either. She looked back at Princess Pyra. She couldn't let her know they hadn't obtained this piece of information until now.

Natascha tried to grab onto something that would get Princess Pyra to do the obstacle course. The obstacle courses were a very important part of The Plan. Without them, The Plan was futile. She snatched a thought.

"We'll kill Helen if you don't do the course," she said darkly.

Pyra twitched. It was very slight and almost imperceptible, but Natascha noticed it. She smiled evilly.

"That's right," Natascha continued. "You don't think you care about her, but deep down you do. And yes, we know you better than you know yourself."

"I don't care what you do to Helen," Pyra retaliated. "She shouldn't be my responsibility anyway."

Some minutes passed as Pyra remain undefeated. Natascha stared her down, hoping she hadn't imagined Pyra's twitch. Her hands became sweaty. She knew if Pyra didn't do the course, then the princess couldn't assimilate into society. The kidnappers needed the princesses to do the course or else The Plan would fail.

Pyra sighed. "Fine, I'll do your stupid course. But only because I know if she's found dead, I could be the one to blame."

"Excellent."

Natascha made a smile that didn't reach her eyes. A weight lifted off her shoulders now that The Plan could continue. Pyra, grimacing, took a starting position.

"Whenever you're ready, you may begin," he said.

Pyra took a quick breath and began running. She didn't mind running through the flames at all. In fact, if made her feel more like she was back at home. She only wished for the ground to be hot as well. Pyra ran over and through many strange objects. She decided it would be smart to gain higher ground. Using flames, she shot herself up to see the course in its entirety. Once she began to get a glimpse of it, a shock ran through her body. She dropped to the ground.

She lay in the heat, the fire slowly reviving her body and soul. *I shouldn't have let a little shock cause me to stop using fire*, she thought. *I must show them they don't have control of me. Rebel. Rebel.*

She stood back up and wiped the blood from her mouth off with the back of her hand. She had fallen from a very high distance. She began running again. She veered off the course and straight into some of the flames. Her captors questioned her; the flames charged her to fight against them.

She looked down at the wristband. She needed to get if off.

Now.

She tried with all her might to pry it off, but it refused to leave its new home on her wrist. Giving up on it for the moment, Pyra flew into the air again with her fire. They weren't going to have power over her any longer. She would fight back. Here and now.

She prepared flames to send toward her captors' separate ways. Once she began to fire, another shock erupted through her body, this one greater than the first. She fell down once again, this time being knocked unconscious.

The captors extinguished the fire then picked up Pyra and took her to the car. They lay her in the back and bound her hands and feet together. They also blindfolded her. He put the seatbelt on Pyra while the female captor started the car. After putting their own seatbelts on, they drove off.

"Did that go as you planned it would?" asked Natascha, who was driving. She said this after some moments of silence.

"Not exactly," he replied. "I knew she would probably retaliate and fight back, and she really was performing the course quite well. I would almost say she'll move on before the others do, but we haven't seen the others yet. I don't want to speak too soon."

The two continued the long drive back.

11

Obstacle Course of Earth

Petunia woke moments before her captors came to get her. They entered the room while she was sitting up, slightly shivering. She obediently allowed them to tie her hands and blindfold her.

"Could you please help me to not fall as we leave?" she politely asked after they had exited the room. "I know the Creator puts trials in our paths, but whenever I do return home, I would rather not be physically changed as much as mentally and spiritually."

Her captors simply looked at each other, confused.

"Are you saying you want us to knock you out?" he asked.

Petunia hung her head and murmured softly, "Do as you wish. Forget I said anything. I live only to serve others. Forgive me, dearest Creator, when I think selfishly. I live only to serve others."

Thus, her captors pressed one of her major arteries, which made her body go limp beneath them. They carried her to the car and drove off.

Petunia almost fell out of the tree but righted herself once she realized where she was. She looked at her surroundings. Below appeared to be the obstacle course she must perform eventually. Above were leaves, and all around her were branches of other trees. She was at the top of an oak tree.

"You awake yet?" a voice from below called. Petunia looked down and saw Natascha. "The obstacle course starts where you're at and continues down here. You may not use your powers to help you during this course lest you wish to be shocked. Whenever you're ready, you may start."

"Thank you!" Petunia replied kindly.

She breathed in and out to prepare herself. She prayed a simple prayer to the Creator for strength and the help to not use her powers. Finally, she stood atop the branch and jumped down, doing a tucked flip. She landed gracefully and hard. Her hand was on the ground for balance.

She stood back up and began running toward the next obstacle of the course. Grabbing the rope, she began the flat, uphill climb. She apologized to the wood underneath her, because she felt no life in it at all. The only time she'd encountered a dead plant was in the room. At the top of the climb, there was a small space, which allowed her to stand.

Tree trunks, and eventually stumps, lay ahead. It looked as if someone had simply cut all but the trunk of the tree off. It nearly brought her to tears to see the trees lying there, dead. Each one was lower than the previous one. Petunia tried to imagine them as stairs or stepping stones. It didn't soothe her heartbreak.

Once she reached the bottom, more logs lay ahead of her. These were simple and rounded, but both the branches and roots had been cut off. She looked over at Natascha who stood off to the side, watching.

"A-am I supposed to step on these poor trees?" Petunia asked.

Natascha only nodded. With eyes filled to the brim with tears, Petunia stepped atop the first log. As she suspected, it rolled beneath her. She stepped onto the next one, then the next, and so on and so forth, and what have she? After that obstacle was complete, she sighed, glad that part was over.

Next was another rope. Seeing as to how it was the only thing that could possibly be next, she began to climb it. At about halfway up, she began slipping. Her body had been sweating from the exercise. Her limbs were not used to this kind of work. She was used to using her mind to control the plants, so they would follow the movements of her body. This was…different. It required a strange level of physical exertion on her part.

Petunia grabbed a better hold of the rope. *One step at a time*, she thought. She placed her right hand above her left and scooted up. She could do this. The Creator was with her, she could feel His presence. Yes, they could do this together.

Quickly she got to the very top and sat there for a moment. She thanked the Creator for His help. The next obstacle was a little distance away. She jumped and caught onto the limb of a tree. Petunia swung herself back and forth, gaining momentum. At what she perceived to be the right moment, she let it go.

The great whoosh of the air on her face was a different thing for her to experience. She closed her eyes. Yes, she'd jumped off trees before, but it never lasted this long. This felt…wrong.

Is this kind of what it's like to be from the Air Kingdom? she wondered.

Smack!

Wise Petunia was not paying attention and also did not realize she had let go just a little too early. She now was sliding down the obstacle, which she was supposed to have landed on. When she reached the solid ground, she tried to stand back up, but the stinging pain was too great.

Natascha had run to Petunia's aid. She commanded, "Don't you dare get up unless you want your injury to worsen."

Petunia obeyed. The male captor came over, gave her a pill and water, and bid her to swallow. She soon felt sleepy, but the pain seemed to have vanished.

Her captors carried her back to the car. They knew by now the pill would have kicked in. Petunia should now be knocked out and her captors able to communicate freely, although they did not speak for a long time. Finally, Natascha broke the silence with a sigh. Her partner spoke.

"What it is?" he said, starting to get worried.

"I just thought," she replied, "at least *one* of them would finish an obstacle course thus far."

He looked down at his hands. "We knew this would be a challenge for them. It shouldn't injure them too much, right?" He looked at her with the most innocent eyes she had ever seen. "I mean, they'll bounce back, right? They'll all be okay? I know medicine's never been my strong suit."

Natascha patted his arm lovingly.

"Look," she said somewhat sternly, "these were just minor wounds they received so far. They shouldn't hurt themselves too badly in these courses. You just keep doing what you've been doing. Okay? You do what you do best. Remember The Plan. As long as we stay the course with that, all will end right and well."

He cheered up a little.

"Yeah, I guess you're right."

The rest of the trek toward the princesses' new home lasted in silence.

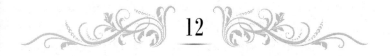

12

Obstacle Course of Air

Cirrus was too tired to notice her captors taking her out of bed. She wondered what was happening in quite a groggy state. She had no idea what was going on, so when she was placed in the vehicle, the leather soft and cushiony, cool air blowing on her face, she fell right back to sleep. Slumber was calling her name. However, right before she fully closed her eyes, she noticed a small emblem in the car. It was an oval crossed over a pickax with a crown behind them both. She didn't find it to be very important.

When her captors noticed Princess Stratus's deep breathing, they wondered if they should give her the shot to knock her out or not. They'd already blindfolded her and bound her wrists. They decided to give her the shot anyway; they would rather be safe than sorry.

Thus, Cirrus woke up much later, wind whipping around her, yet she could not feel said wind; she could only hear it. She sat in an upright position and found Natascha in this dreary place.

"Where am I?" she asked. It was an innocent and simple question, especially for Stratus. "And what are we in?"

"We are flying in a helicopter and have almost arrived to your obstacle course," replied Natascha.

Cirrus made a *tch* sound.

"You call *this* flying? Ha!" she challenged. "You petty criminals have no idea what it's like to fly in the air."

"Well," Natascha continued, "Why don't you show us? Unlike the others, you may not start whenever. Once we fly past it, it's too much trouble to turn back around, so you must start in exactly 59 seconds and counting.

"Also, you are not allowed to use your powers. Enjoy."

Natascha finished getting ready to jump out while keeping a close eye on Princess Stratus. She put a backpack on as well as goggles. Cirrus thought Natascha's attire was very strange indeed. Nothing seemed to make sense to Stratus anymore. Her captors were most definitely a strange people.

Cirrus perked up when she heard a door fling open; air whooshed inside. It felt most wonderful.

"Ten seconds!" Natascha yelled and began counting backward. "Nine!"

Cirrus looked down. This was a very strange land, she decided. When she got back, she would tell the others about all she saw since she remembered everything. She might as well at least try to escape.

Stratus wasn't ready for Natascha's push out of the helicopter. Immediately, Cirrus righted herself with air to get a better view of the obstacle course.

This was not a good idea, she soon found out.

She was greeted by a shock powerful enough to knock the wind out of her and caused her to lose concentration on her powers.

Seeing a hoop, she grabbed onto it and sat. It immediately began to sink, and thus she used it to ricochet herself onto another hoop nearby. This time, she expected it to act as the first had, and she was right. Two or so more hoops lay ahead of her.

This is easy! she thought to herself as she landed onto a solid platform. She looked back. *I could do that all day! So much for obstacles! Did they really think that for someone from the Air Kingdom, a princess no less, this wouldn't even be considered remotely hard?*

As she looked forward, her smirk began to fade. The next part could easily be done by controlling the air, but that shock was not pleasant whatsoever. She wasn't sure if she was willing to experience it again. She looked down. She *could* jump off the platform and attempt to escape, but…

Stratus looked over at Natascha who also stood on the platform.

"What will happen if I try to escape?" Cirrus asked.

"You will be shocked," replied Natascha blatantly.

"Hm…"

"You are being timed, you realize?"

"Oh." Stratus looked down. "What is this place like of which you call home? I know it's nothing compared to my kingdom, but this way, I can at least contrast how much better the Air Kingdom is."

Natascha said nothing in reply. Cirrus looked at the task ahead. It consisted of an expanse of nothingness. There was another platform in fifty yards. She could not jump across it, nor could she use her powers lest she ask for pain throughout her limbs.

"How am I expected to cross this?" Stratus asked. Natascha did not reply once again. Cirrus sighed and jumped.

As she fell she saw a seemingly small object. She stared at it as it became bigger and bigger, closer and closer. She aimed for her feet to hit it as a landing. She was surprised when she bounced upward, and it caused her to lose her balance. The second platform was near to her, and she reached up toward it with her hand. When she began to fall back down, she pushed the air under her feet to raise her. Once she crawled atop of the platform, she received another shock.

She looked back at Natascha as she stood up, grimacing. Before her now were triangular handles, but she had to jump in order to reach the first. Then something else unexpected happened. The handle began to rise, fast.

She reached for the second one with her feet then hung upside down. Soon enough, she could reach the third handle with her hands. For now, she stuck with this process. There were eleven handles that sloped downward, thus, making it all that much more difficult to execute.

After the last handle was a long, thin platform and was the width of one of Stratus's feet. Once she landed, her feet slipped, and she fell off. She allowed her body to fall, thinking this was a wonderful thing. It was like flying, but with much, much less effort. She was lying on her back, her legs crossed, arms behind her head, and eyes closed. This was probably one of the most relaxing things she'd ever done. She wasn't worried about hitting the ground for she was high up, and she could easily save herself whenever the time came.

She landed sooner than she expected. She opened her eyes since air was still rushing around her but now in the opposing direction. Natascha was holding her and taking her toward the helicopter. Cirrus was very upset.

"Unhand me, woman!" she screeched. "How dare you touch *me,* the Air princess! You just wait until my parents hear about this! You will surely be murdered in the town square, and everyone will be required to watch the death of you evildoers! Just you wait! You shall rue the day you ever even *thought* about kidnapping me!"

Natascha was silent in reply. She had realized a while ago it was simply better to say nothing than to give out some piece of information by accident lest it aid the prisoners' escape. Stratus crossed her arms and turned her head away with a huff.

Eventually they arrived at the helicopter, and Cirrus was injected once again

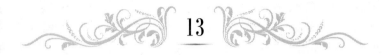

13

Obstacle Course of Water

Cirrus returned late that night. Currentide felt her presence and was awakened. She made note of Stratus's weak state of mind. She wondered what Cirrus went through that day and what she would have to go through when it was her turn.

She tried to reach the minds of those back home, but her ability could not reach that far. She hadn't trained in distance as much as she should have. She instead paid more attention to unlocking closed minds, blocking hers from others, as well as controlling others' decisions and thoughts. Currentide wanted some form of homely comfort (for example, messing with Flowon), but even that had been taken away by her captors.

She tossed and turned throughout the rest of the night. When the captors came in the early morning, she was easily taken, somewhat glad to leave this room, which was becoming all too familiar.

Immediately after leaving the room, her captors blindfolded her and tied her hands behind her back. They led her, and she was slowly dragged along. She desperately wished her ability allowed her to see what was literally around her, but alas, it only allowed her to look into minds. It did not register objects without thought.

She was placed in an odd object and a flat protection device placed across her. They forced a drink into her mouth, and she had no other choice but to drink it. The liquid flowed throughout her body, and unconsciousness reigned supreme over her.

She awoke to the sounds of crashing waves. Her bonds were there no longer. Slowly, she sat up and looked around. She was completely surrounded by water. Knowing full well it wasn't her water, she was excited nonetheless. She looked at where she lay and felt the grains of sand under her arms and legs.

"Now that you've seen the beginning of your obstacle course," Natascha said. "We'll explain the rules to you again."

Both Natascha and the other captor wore skintight suits, giant fins on their feet, and large capsules on their backs. Personally, Currentide thought they looked silly. She laughed internally at them. Wouldn't it be easier to simply swim without all of the strange equipment?

"Once again, if you try to use your powers you will be shocked."

Currentide thought while Natascha said this. She recalled reading something about electricity and water. She thought the book had said something about electricity sparking in water or sending its energy waves throughout the body of water, or something like that. When she had read the book, she had also wondered about this thing called electricity since she had never heard of it before but could find no other mention of the topic. She figured she might as well test her captors to see if this information was true.

"Wouldn't the electricity fizz out in the water or send its waves throughout the water?"

Natascha sighed. These girls had such little knowledge of places outside their own kingdoms.

"Each of the wristbands is custom-made for each obstacle course. For example, yours is waterproof, meaning it can withstand water. It has also been made so if we shock you, it will only shock you and won't touch the water around you."

Currentide mulled over this piece of information, although not for long since Natascha interrupted Currentide's thoughts with more information.

"The obstacle course lies underneath the water. We will be surveying you the entire time, so don't try to escape. We know the area better than you do, so even if you tried to, we would capture you again."

Currentide eyed her captors. They really didn't want her to leave, but what would they do if she attempted to? She kind of wanted to find out.

"When you're ready, you may begin," the male captor said as he put on a mask.

Immediately, Currentide gracefully dived into the water. The captors followed closely behind. Currrentide looked around and saw schools of fish. She commanded them to come to her nonchalantly. Soon enough, she was surrounded by fish; the schools were so thick and plentiful the captors could not see Currentide through them.

The captors began to worry themselves, thinking she was trying to escape. Natascha sent a strong shock to Currentide's wristband. Currentide cried out in excruciating pain. The male captor flinched at her cry; he never wanted the girls to get hurt but knew it was necessary in order for The Plan to work.

The fish lifted Currentide's limp body. The captors attempted to take Currentide's body from the fish, but the fish retaliated and attacked them since they hadn't received a new command. The captors swam back a little to survey the scene. The fish began to carry Currentide's body away. Both captors looked at each other and nodded. They must get Princess Currentide back, even at the expense of their physical condition.

They swam hard and fast toward Currentide and the fish. The fish were getting farther and farther away; the captors couldn't let them take Princess Currentide. He signed to Natascha that he would go get the boat, and she should go after the princess. They could meet up and overpower them, together. Natascha nodded. This plan could work; it had to work. They had to get her back.

So Natascha swam furiously after Princess Currentide. She hadn't taken swim in school for nothing. She was also much more athletic than her partner in crime, which they both knew.

The other captor was doing his best to swim quickly, although he was athletic by no means. He was mainly used to working at a sit-down job where he generated new ideas. Kidnapping the princesses was one of the most exhausting pieces of work he had ever done, but without the princesses, The Plan would never work. They needed to assimilate into society.

He reached the ladder of the boat and climbed up. The boat was settled near the island which Currentide awoke upon. He took off his mask for maximum sight and breathing. The key was already in the ignition, so all he had to do was fire up the boat and go. This he did.

Even though his athleticism was terrible, his sense of direction was amazing. He moved the boat at a high speed toward the direction the fish were headed. He went quite a ways before he saw Natascha's head pop out of the water. He turned the boat off, put his mask back on, grabbed the net with large holes, and dived in. Natascha had gone under as well. When he could see well he gave Natascha the thumbs-up. She pointed down below them, where the fish carried Currentide toward some underwater tunnels. The two captors swam down toward the fish, net spread between them. They knew they must recapture Currentide, at any and all costs.

So they swam to the fish. The fish, and therefore Currentide, were about to enter the tunnels when the captors captured them all in the net. Currentide broke from her unconscious state and looked around her once again. The fish, feeling she was awake and having no current command, were smart and swam out of the net. Currentide saw her captors and crossed her arms with a huff. Just as she was commanding more creatures of the sea to obey her will, Natascha knocked her out with an air tank.

Quickly, the captors swam up to the boat and headed back to the place of the princess's imprisonment.

"Hey," he yelled over the wind. He was driving at max speed for the fun of it. He continued on, but it was lost in the air.

"What?" Natascha yelled back.

"CAN YOU BELIEVE THE WATER PRINCESS TRIED TO ESCAPE?"

Natascha thought for a moment. Princess Pyra did not surprise her, but Princess Currentide seemed to be more shy. Of course, they could never know what was going on in any of their heads. Natascha voiced her thoughts to her fellow captor.

He knew they must start watching them more carefully from now on, for many things could happen in these obstacle courses.

14

Discussions

Natascha and the other captor, David, were in the monitoring room after dropping off Currentide to her room. It was late at night, and the kidnappers were exhausted. They turned to the giant monitor and watched the princesses in their terrible housing.

"Incoming video chat," a voice resounded. "Accept or reject?"

David looked at the screen. He said, "Accept."

A face appeared on the large monitor. The princesses were transferred to several smaller screens which surrounded the large one. Natascha and David easily recognized the man. They'd known about him for years and were very grateful to be in his service.

"How is it coming?" the face asked. "Are they…?"

Natascha nodded. "We have the princesses."

A big smile spread across his pudgy face. "Oh good! Are they all right? They aren't too much trouble, are they?"

"Well, two have tried to esca—"

"No, not at all," Natascha interrupted David. "They've been very good princesses. I'm sure they'll be ready soon enough."

The man on the screen relaxed visibly. "Oh good, because I would really hate it if one of them got away."

David cringed away. Now his leader's happiness depended on how good of a job he did. David did not want to see his superior become furious. He couldn't bear the thought of it.

"I'll make sure they stay here until you ask to see them," David assured the leader.

The leader nodded. "I have some preparations to make before they arrive. I'll send the fifth princess when the time comes. Until then I require you to keep them in good health. Feed them well and keep their hygiene in good condition. I can't handle unhygienic guests. It's just gross. I also don't want them to be scared of you either."

Natascha nodded at the orders. "We'll make sure to do that."

She decided it was best not to tell their superior about the princesses's lack of need to eat and other basic health needs. What he didn't know wouldn't hurt him. Right now, Natascha found it unnecessary to inform him of this. He'd find out sooner or later.

"Is there anything else we need to know?" David questioned. With the princesses having just finished the obstacle courses, David and Natascha had some discussing to do. Not a single one had completed a course. Their hopes were higher for these princesses.

"Yes," the face on the screen said. "Tell me what the princesses are like. No, wait. Don't tell me I want to find out...but I really want to know now! What do you think, Natascha?"

"I think you should know what they're like now," she said without hesitation. Sure, their superior was obviously giddy about seeing the princesses, but Natascha thought he should be prepared for when that day came.

The leader was silent for a small moment. "What do you think, David?"

David said nothing for some time. He knew what he thought but was afraid to voice it for he knew the trouble it could bring. He was silent for too long, and his superior took notice.

"What is it, David?" he interrogated. "Surely you have an opinion on the matter. I order you to tell me your thoughts! I will not sit through your indecisiveness. Tell me now, or I will tear your reputation to pieces! And don't lie to me!"

David's eyes widened. "I honestly don't think you should know about the princesses's personalities yet."

"I'm sorry, but apparently there is something we need to discuss without you," Natascha persuaded. "It's nothing you said. David and I simply need to see things in the same light."

Before their superior could say anything, she temporarily stopped the video chat.

"What did I say?" David asked.

"Can you imagine the reaction our majestic leader will be put through if he doesn't know now?" Natascha retaliated. "He'll go into shock from the onslaught!"

"If he finds out what the princesses are like right now, he may change his mind," David growled. "We'll have to take the princesses back to their kingdoms. I don't want all that we've done to go to waste. All our efforts can't be for nothing!"

"Fine!"

Natascha and David sat in silence for some time.

"How about a compromise?" Natascha suggested. "We'll tell him about the princesses one by one. We won't tell him about all of them just yet. We'll stretch them throughout our video chats. Then he won't be completely upset when he finds out how…undesirable some of them are."

"Fine," David agreed. "But who should we tell him about first?"

Natascha thought for some minutes as did David.

"Petunia," they said simultaneously. And so it was decided.

Natascha quickly resumed the video chat.

"You better have a good explanation for this!" their superior said, furious.

"We've decided to tell you about a princess," David said.

"A decision couldn't have been that hard to make!"

"We'll tell you about another one at our next video chat. We'll then tell you about a third then the fourth."

"Hmph. I'm definitely not giving you a raise now."

Natascha rolled her eyes. Her leader often threatened he wasn't going to give them a raise, but it's not like he ever gave them raises, anyway.

"Now tell me about this princess," the superior said.

"She's from the Earth Kingdom," David said. "Her name is Princess Petunia."

"Princess Petunia…" the leader echoed.

"She's very sweet and kind, always thinking of others instead of herself."

The superior smiled. Natascha continued where David left off. "She's not very good in a fight and hates conflict. She'd rather resolve a problem than start one."

"So she's a peacemaker?" the man on the screen asked. Natascha nodded. The leader's face immediately relaxed. "Tell me more."

"She's not very strong. She couldn't hurt someone even if she wanted. I don't think I've ever seen her get angry. David?"

David shook his head. "She's never been angry even when anyone else would have been. She's patient with everyone."

"She sounds wonderful," the leader said.

Within minutes, they heard a snoring sound. Their superior's eyes were closed. Natascha and David looked at each other. They shut off communication with the man on the screen and thought going to sleep sounded like a good idea.

15

Varying Thoughts

A shrill whistle woke them all up from their not-exactly-comfortable beds. Pyra didn't move.

"Shut up!" Pyra yelled. "Who in their right mind would even dare to wake me up? I've barely gotten any sleep in this forsaken place. If you even had a sliver of kindness you'd wait until I woke up *on my own time*."

"Tch," Natascha replied. "If we waited until then, nothing would ever get done. Now get up."

Pyra shot up and looked around herself frantically.

"What in the world just happened?" she exclaimed. She looked over and saw Natascha. Pyra pointed accusingly. "You! You did this to me! You awoke me from my blissful dream where I was terrorizing evil kidnappers who take my sleep away."

Natascha sidestepped Pyra's oncoming punch, followed by a roundhouse kick. She grabbed Pyra's foot as Pyra was about to slam her foot atop Natascha's shoulder.

"I did nothing to you," Natascha said coldly. "All I did was blow the whistle."

"Liar!" Pyra yanked her foot out of Natascha's grip and brought it back to the ground. She folded her arms. "There was no whistle. You did some kind of voodoo magic to make me wake up! I felt it in my bones and mind. You can't deny what you did!"

Natascha merely shook her head. Pyra was greatly mistaken. Natascha looked at the other girls.

"Meet outside the room in five minutes."

With that, she turned on her heel and escaped the room, leaving the door slightly ajar. The princesses looked at each other, except Pyra was looking anywhere but. She was very upset with her captors.

First, they put her in a cold, enclosed space with these lunatics. How could she ever survive? Second, they made her do some obstacle course and shocked her. Enough said. And finally, they kept messing with her head, when all she wanted to do was sleep peacefully for one night. Was that so much to ask?

Quickly Cirrus, Petunia, and Currentide left the room. Pyra stayed behind for a few moments. She was starting to get angry and needed to get it out fast. Good things never transpired because of Pyra's anger.

She stepped onto her continually burning bed. It was holding its shape surprisingly well. Pyra proceeded to punch the wall as if it was a punching bag. Blood thickly covered her hands. At first, the blows hurt. Eventually it became a tingle, and she became immune to it.

Her frustration out, she commanded fire to appear as a coating over her hands. Within the next few minutes, the damage she had created had been undone. Her hands no longer hurt and were completely healed.

"I told you five minutes!" Natascha yelled as she dragged Pyra out of the room.

"You do realize I was about to come out, right?" she answered with a raised eyebrow.

"When I say five minutes," growled Natascha in reply, "I mean five minutes."

And thus Pyra was dragged out of the room. Pyra was very unhappy about all this and grumbled the entire excursion. Natascha dropped her off by the other princesses who were gathered by the male captor who was pacing. The light was still on, although they knew what he looked like now. Natascha took her position off to the side.

"I can't believe you girls," he said. "None of you managed to complete the course, not a single one." He stopped pacing. "Now why is that?"

Petunia and Cirrus shuffled their feet a little. Natascha internally swelled with pride. Her partner was becoming great at basically denying his whole self and acting for these princesses. Rather than the shy, introverted guy she'd come to know, he became stern and ironhanded. It wasn't as hard for Natascha to treat the princesses like she did, but she could only wonder what it was like for him to become this other person.

"I am most disappointed," he continued, "that a couple of you tried to escape. The other two maneuvered the obstacle courses well but failed to complete them too.

"Today, you will be locked in your room after this meeting. Tomorrow, the door will be opened. It is set to lock once it is closed. You will be free to roam the building. Understand that I am giving you this grace although you don't deserve it. Earlier this week, the door was unlocked by accident. You explored. This was a fault on our part, so we locked it back, but two of you remained outside. We then had to unlock it once again. Do not try to escape again. You should not depend upon this fault nor expect it in the future. Are we clear?"

The girls nodded.

"You are free to go back to your room."

They walked the minute or so back. They all sat on their respective beds. Pyra lay down on her flames, ready to go back to sleep. She was sincerely going to attempt anyway. It would be a lot easier if Stratus and Petunia stopped talking. Try as she might it became hard to fall asleep.

"Currentide, I have to know," Cirrus said. "What was your obstacle course like?"

Everyone else had relayed their obstacle courses the day following their obstacle course. They were all in the dark about one recall. Currentide did not know about Pyra's,

Cirrus didn't know about Petunia's, Petunia didn't know about Pyra's, and no one knew about Currentide's yet. This only happened because each told her story the day after it happened.

Now it was Currentide's turn to tell her tale. She merely shrugged.

"Oh, c'mon!" Cirrus argued. "There has to be *something* you want to tell us."

Currentide rolled over, so she faced the wall. Petunia burst into tears.

"What?" said Stratus, soundly slightly annoyed.

"It's just that," she started, "seeing those poor, dead, and abandoned trees the other day broke my heart. That was one reason I hadn't finished the course. I couldn't think of any person who would willingly destroy the precious life which the Creator has so graciously given us."

At this, Pyra raised her hand. She said, "I would."

Petunia gasped.

"P-Pyra!" she exclaimed. "H-h-how could you d-do such a th-thing?"

Pyra sat up, knowing she would get no more sleep until tonight.

"Petunia, you are the dumbest person I know," she said with utmost sincerity. She also said these words slowly. "I say this with all the patience I have. In case you haven't noticed, I'm from the *Fire* Kingdom. My kingdom would turn yours into ashes within seconds."

As she pretended to be Petunia, she placed her voice up a couple octaves and very bubbly.

"This is when you say, 'Wow, Pyra! I never knew any of this information before! Thank you *so* much for enlightening me. Now I can return to the sunshine and rainbows, which are my life!' Well, you probably should say it with easier, smaller words since I'm pretty sure words like 'to' and 'I' may be too hard for you."

Pyra lay back down and once again tried to fall asleep. Petunia was nearly in tears.

"I forgive you, Pyra," she said so quietly it was almost inaudible. "I forgive you and will continue to love you and the others."

Then Petunia, too, lay down on her bed and prayed to the Creator.

Dearest Creator, she pleaded. *Why have You put me here with these people? I know You have good reasons and intentions, but I pray You can truly enlighten me as to what we're doing here. Why would the four of us ever come together? We don't get along too well, although I've been sincerely trying. What kind of test is this? I know it's not right to question Your great plan for each and every one of us, but I just needed to voice my thoughts to someone. Thank You for listening. I'll try to disturb You no more.*

Cirrus was unsure what to do. She looked over at Currentide and sighed. There was no hope in trying to talk with her. So Stratus walked over to the mirror. She fingered her hair with her hands, releasing the knots out of it. She was obviously the most beautiful one here.

No, you're not, a small voice told her.

Cirrus's eyes grew wide. No, it wouldn't come again, not this year. She refused to allow it to overcome her. She would fight, yes. She could easily do that, right? A chill overcame her.

She looked back at the mirror and saw her twin staring at her. She reached up to touch her hand. Her reflection followed suit.

If only she was still here, she thought. *Would we have been kidnapped together? What kind of a person would I be? Would we cause trouble in defiance of the kingdom, shouting that we would be both rule it together? Would she be stuck in a room somewhere, learning all she'd need to know in order to rule the kingdom properly?*

A tear threatened to escape, but she commanded it back to stay in her eye.

You always were the smart one. I-if you hadn't been murdered...

No, she refused to ask *that* question. She couldn't think of herself that way when she never had a choice when it happened. Stratus looked over at Currentide then went to her bed. Cirrus wept heartily for her twin. Yes, she must continue to keep this a secret from everyone.

For her twin's sake.

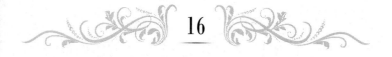

16

A Few Days Ago

Many citizens were requested to enter the queens and kings' presence. This was because the kings and queens were questioning the last people who had seen their children.

One of these concerned persons was Flowon. Being her personal attendant, he was the most obvious person to know the events leading up to Currentide's kidnapping. He was in their majesties' presence the day Currentide was reported missing.

"Flowon," King Mul's voice boomed out. "First, we would like to hear this conversation audibly. Second, you are required to know where Currentide is at all times, correct?"

"Yes, sir," came Flowon's reply. "To both, sir."

Would he get fired for not knowing where Currentide was now? He earnestly hoped he didn't. He didn't know what kind of position he would acquire if he was to be fired. All he'd ever done was watch Currentide and follow her around. He didn't think there were many jobs, if any at all, of which this set of skills would come in handy.

"Shall we assume you currently do not know where she is?" Queen Mizu asked with a laugh.

"Yes, ma'am."

"Well, it was worth a shot," said King Mul. The couple laughed. Flowon thought about how perfect they were together. The previous rulers had done a good job in picking a spouse for their heir. King Mul continued, "Could you relay the events of the day Princess Currentide disappeared?"

"Well, Your Highness, she took a long time that morning to get ready. I stood outside at this time. I dragged her to water class. The teacher was good and patient. Afterward she said she had to use the restroom, so I allowed her to do so. I sat down as I waited for her return."

Flowon sighed then continued.

"I waited an hour before I suspected her trickery. I apologize for not being alert as I should have been. I asked around if anyone had seen her. I searched for hours. She had already missed half of her next class before I looked out in the streets. I found her off to the side of a crowd and reprimanded her for swimming off. We argued a bit, and eventually, I dragged her to her class.

"I apologize for leaving her, but after dropping her off, I went to get a snack. When I came back, she'd made another teacher quit outright. This was Ms. Whiteside who had quit. Afterward, we went to the royal library and remained there until she disappeared."

"Relay what you saw," Queen Mizu commanded.

"Yes, Your Highness.

"A kidnapping might have begun in the library, but I am unsure. It could have happened a little later. It was getting late, so I ordered Princess Currentide to put her books away, and she obliged. When she came back, a strange person was holding her."

"Describe this person," demanded King Mul.

"Yes, Your Majesty. It, I'm unsure of the person's gender, was in dark clothes that were skintight. It also had a cylinder upon its back. It had fins on its feet and gloves on its hands. It had a mask on. This is all I noticed in the midst of the danger.

"It told me Princess Currentide had fainted unexpectedly. Its voice gurgled and was unidentifiable. I was leading it to the doctor when I lost it. I do not know at what time it left, but I didn't notice the loss of its presence until I said we only had a few more hallways left. It did not reply, so I turned around and stopped. It was no longer there. I do not know if it kidnapped the princess or if it was kidnapped with the princess, if there was a kidnapping at all. I searched the castle all night. Her maids said she had not come to her room. It was then that we reported Princess Currentide was missing."

"What was this possible kidnapper's mind like?" asked Queen Mizu.

"Forgive me, Your Majesties, but I did not think to search his or her mind in the midst of everything."

"That would have been the princess's *first* thing to do," grumbled King Mul.

"Forgi—"

"No!" shouted the king who banged his fist on his chair. "Servant Flowon, make it your duty to find and rescue the princess!"

"Y-yes, sir!"

"Dismissed!" Queen Mizu said.

Flowon left as quickly as possible, thinking all the while indeed how he would rescue Currentide.

King Hwajae punched the wall as hard as possible. It was a trait that ran through the family. Queen Kasai simply stood off to the side, arms crossed.

"You realize punching that wall isn't going to get our daughter back, right?" she said.

"Of course, I realize that!" he retaliated hotly. "I'm just so angry!"

"And you don't think I am? You don't think I want to find our daughter, the *heir*, as much as you do?"

"I know you do, but the easiest way to get rid of my anger is through violence. You know that."

The queen flipped her hair out of her eyes and sighed. If only it were easier. The king punched the wall again and looked out a window.

The queen and king had been frantically searching for their daughter. They'd sent guards and servants all across the kingdom searching for Princess Pyra with no luck. The last to see her appeared to be the head chef and Helen. The maid Pyra'd known since childhood reported the absence of Pyra the morning after her disappearance. When the rulers required all who had seen the princess the day she'd disappeared into their presence, very few came. It was very much like Princess Pyra to mostly keep to herself throughout the day.

It mainly upset the rulers simply because they had seen her on that day. They also knew whoever had taken, or worse killed, Pyra was strong since they had trained their daughter to fight any perpetrator. Not that she wouldn't have done that of her own free will.

Where are you my daughter? the king thought to himself. *Where have you gone? Come back the castle. Escape if you have been taken. If you were murdered…*

The Air Kingdom figured they would find the princess easily, seeing as how they remembered everything. The queen and king called Cirrus's maid and butler into their presence.

"Tell us yesterday's events leading up to when the princess was reported to have disappeared," said King Gong-Gi.

"I woke up at—"

"Summarize as best as you can," Queen Kūki said gently.

Both nodded. Sometimes when an order was given by the queen or king, it went for both of them. Miguel the butler began speaking.

"That morning began as usual. I believe Marai tended Princess Stratus as usual. The princess came out early that morning saying she was ready to go to class. This surprised me, but I guided her there nonetheless. When we arrived, she said to me, 'You are free to go now. Send Marai when class is over.' I replied with, 'As you wish, Princess.' After that, I left to relay the message."

The maid Marai continued their tale from there, her thick accent protruding.

"I went'a to her classroom just'a before its usual ending time when her teacher informed me Princess Cirrus was not'a there. He, the instructor, said she had never even come to class! I left'a to question Miguel about it. He told me he *had* delivered the princess to class! So we'a had to search the castle for her. During this we found out'a Your Great Majesties needed her for the dinner party that'a night'a and all of the decisions the princess needed to make for her coronation day.

"At'a this point, Miguel and I began searching much more rigorously. We finally found her at the track with some other whippersnappers about her age. She was speaking with a commonboy whom I've never met'a before. The Princess Cirrus came quicker than I expected. We then brought her to the ballroom where she made coronation day decisions."

Miguel continued the tale.

"As soon as she was finished, we took her to her room to prepare for that evening's dinner party. Then we took her to the dinner and left. She returned to her room that night where Marai finished Princess Stratus for the day. We proceeded to head to our own quarters for the night. This morning we reported her missing."

"She was most definitely there last night'a, sire," Marai said.

The king leaned back in his throne.

"Very well," he said. "Your services are no longer required."

With a wave of his hand, he dismissed them. The queen and king were alone after they dismissed the other servants as well. They sat in silence for a long time, pondering what to do next. Queen Kūki broke the silence.

"How can a kingdom, the *Air Kingdom* especially, lose a princess?"

King Gong-Gi simply rested his head on his hands and ran those hands through his hair. It was a simple question they couldn't answer. The wisest choice would be to ask the

Earth Kingdom, the wisest of them all, what they thought. But pride in the summer commanded the Air Kingdom to not seek help.

King Jigu and Queen Chikyū were scatterbrained. Where was their daughter? It was most unlike her to simply run away. If someone had found her surely they would return her? Unless she was running away from something, and the people, out of kindness, wanted to keep her safe. What if it was too dangerous to even send a message? Was that what happened? Or had their daughter been kidnapped or murdered?

At this last thought, they really started to worry. Who would kill Princess Petunia?

Once the news of their missing daughter reached their ears, the queen and king sent servants to search the castle, and they searched the towns nearby. They immediately asked almost all the townsfolk they saw. All were very helpful and kind to their rulers.

Their search led them to a local bakery.

"Oh, Mrs. Jenny!" King Jigu exclaimed.

"King Jigu," she said quietly and gasped, causing her bowl to crash to the ground.

Queen Chikyū began cleaning up the shattered remnants while her husband and Jenny DuBois talked.

"Do you have any idea what might have happened to my daughter, Princess Petunia?" said the king. "We haven't seen her since yesterday; she never came home."

"Sh-she was just helping me out," Mrs. Jenny DuBois replied.

"Please, can you tell me what happened that day?"

"Y-yes, Your Majesty. Well, you see, Your Highness, she usually helps me out, but that day chickens were everywhere. She got the boy responsible for it to clean it up. After that she left. I sent her to get flour, but the boy came back with it saying he was the one who did everything. It was perfect, just the way I like it. I asked him why Petunia—oh, I'm sorry, my deepest apologies—Princess Petunia hadn't bought it, and he said she had some other errand to run. I paid him, and he was off. He most definitely didn't do it! He's much too young to pull off a stunt like stealing the princess. He's one of us and shouldn't dare even think of it!"

King Jigu grabbed Mrs. DuBois's hands.

"Thank you for your information," he said. "I know it will be helpful to us in the long run."

With that, he and his wife left in search of the next place their daughter went. Locals helped them find the path. Eventually their search led them to a shabby shack. Queen Chikyū looked worriedly at her husband and tentatively knocked on the door. A gruff man opened it.

"Yes?" he growled.

"Um, pardon our rudeness," said the queen. "But our daughter is missing. Some other citizens of this town led our search to you. Could you please help us?"

"If you think she's in here, she's not. You have to realize I meet many students throughout the week. I can't simply know who your daughter is."

King Jigu didn't want to play the royalty card, but it seemed like their only option left. He looked at the ground, as if ashamed to admit it.

"Excuse me," he mumbled, "but I don't know all that our daughter told you, but she's Princess Petunia, and we really need to get her back."

At this, the gruff man's eyes widened in shock. He bowed low.

"I'm terribly sorry I didn't notice the resemblance earlier." He stood back up. "It is an honor to meet you. If you wouldn't mind coming in for a bit of tea I can bring you up to speed as far as what I know of your daughter. Maybe I can be some kind of useful to you."

The rulers of the Earth Kingdom walked into the shack. There wasn't much light or room, but he had managed to scrounge out three chairs. Or forms of chairs. The owner ended up sitting on a barrel, and the king and queen were on stools. Once the tea was ready, he began telling what he knew of the missing princess.

"My name is Yao-Lin Sruli. Most of my students simply call me Mr. Sruli. Your daughter is exceptional with her powers, she is my best student, in fact. Um, not that the others aren't exceptional as well. They're good too. Recently, we were having a lesson—I have lessons in a nearby field. Petunia got caught up in her powers. The plants began wrapping around her. She lost control, and they gained it from her.

"I noticed the danger and built a cage of my own plants around her, fighting control against them."

At this, he took a sip of his tea. He took a few more sips slowly. He liked to do things on his own time. His tea was three-fourths full at this point. He continued the story.

"I placed the princess in her cage off to the side and focused on the plant problem she created. I first tried to coax them out of the trance she had put them in. When that didn't work, I tried to fight them with my own plants. I felt like I was simply stalling them. I knew that if I left her, the plants would overtake her, and she would become one with the Earth. I felt, though, she should be allowed to keep living, so I kept fighting.

"I prayed to the Creator to send someone to help me. I knew I couldn't do it on my own. At that point, one of my students showed up. He is the worst student a teacher could ask for, but he tries so hard. If the rest of my students tried as hard as he does…" He said he came just so he could practice for our lesson later that day. He then realized the problem at hand. He asked if he could help.

"I said, 'If you can think of something I have yet to do, then go for it.' He said, 'Okay.' I didn't think he could be any kind of help.

"Somehow, I still don't how it was possible, but somehow he managed to fend off the plants. He acted as if it was no big deal when it was most definitely something I never would have expected from him.

"I stood there in shock for a few minutes just wondering how it was possible. I looked around me, trying to seek the Creator, although I knew I wouldn't see Him. I sent Him a prayer of thanks and finished the task at hand.

"I went over to the princess and uncaged my plants from her. I asked my pupil if he would take me to the local hospital, and he did. I was carrying the princess. I apologize for taking her without her permission."

Queen Chikyū just smiled and said, "As long as we get her back all is fine. You did what you had to. I'd rather her be safe than you worry about some conduct."

"Thank you. Once at the hospital, I thanked my student for his help and dismissed him. I talked to the receptionist who led me into a vacant room. I laid your daughter on the bed and waited until a doctor came. He took care of her, and I waited near the receptionist until I was allowed to see her again.

"Normally, I would have found the family and told them, but she never told me any of that. She kept quiet about it all and seemed determined to not let me know.

"Once I was allowed back in her room, I waited there for hours. A nurse came in, saying that visiting hours were over. I reluctantly left, hoping she was in very capable hands. I went about my usual life after that."

"That's quite a tale you have," King Jigu said.

The trio sat in silence for some time before Mr. Sruli spoke up.

"Was she reported missing after that day?"

"Yes," came Queen Chikyū's quiet voice.

"That means I'm your number one suspect, right?"

The queen did not reply, but she got up and left. Her husband followed suit after thanking Mr. Sruli for his help.

17

Pyra's Struggle

"Are you sure you guys don't need showers?" Natascha asked for the umpteenth time. "You've been here for nearly four weeks."

The princesses groaned again. Natascha was always asking them the same questions about food, water, and hygiene. However, now they were getting braver and wittier in their replies. They'd realized that as long as they did the obstacle courses their captors were happy, *and* they were allowed a day to explore. This they took greedily. On each exploration, they gained more and more knowledge. Currentide once dragged Cirrus to the library and forced her to look at every book since Stratus would remember it. She accomplished this using her mind ability, of course. Stratus was mad afterward since she understood nothing she saw. It was written in another language.

In the past weeks a couple of them, Pyra and Currentide, realized that they *could* use their powers as long as it blended in with the rest of the element. Their captors appeared unable to tell the difference, unlike those from the Fire and Water Kingdoms. On the other hand, Cirrus and Petunia didn't dare to use their powers for fear of being shocked.

Pyra was always the first to reply as usual. This time, she balanced out her options with her hands, making Natascha appear less knowledgeable.

"Uh, water…" Pyra lifted one hand. "Douses fire." Pyra lifted her other hand and began balancing the invisible objects. "Hm…tough call."

"I'm honestly used to just blowing the stink off of me," Stratus said haughtily. "We also have the best and most voluminous collection of perfumes available in the Air Kingdom."

"Well," said Petunia in all seriousness, "when one is surrounded by plants and earth, one needn't take showers since we wish to become one with the earth one day. If earth only takes showers whenever rain falls, which doesn't happen often, and then it is used as a drink, then why should we shower?"

Natascha began rubbing her forehead. The more comfortable these princesses got, the more they gave her headaches. At least they were doing the obstacle courses now, however. That was what they needed them to do for part one of The Plan, and thus it was mostly what they cared about.

"Princess Currentide," she said, "do you have anything you'd like to add? Maybe another retort or something or other?"

"I-I wasn't retorting," Petunia said quietly, but no one paid any attention to her. They were all focused on whether Currentide would speak or not; she seldom did.

Internally Currentide was simply wondering what she should do. She wanted to say something but didn't want to give the others the pleasure of her retorting with them. She refused to retaliate with them and knew if they weren't here she would reply. She knew exactly what she wanted to say. She would start with "I was constantly surrounded by water in the Water Kingdom." Then she would add "Do you really think we took showers?" or maybe "How would I know if I needed to shower or not?"

She couldn't quite decide which, but she knew she needed to be quiet if she wanted to keep her mysteriousness up.

So with some regret, she remained silent. Natascha sighed and continued.

"Well, whatever," she said. "If you need anything, you know what to do: just say it, and we'll decide how to respond."

Natascha left and closed the door. This was one of the days where they simply sat in their room all day. It wasn't exciting, and they'd tried to escape before, but their captors found out within seconds. They hadn't really tried since. Now they all sat on their beds, the most comfortable items in the room, which wasn't saying much.

Cirrus's back was facing everyone else. In the past few weeks, she'd grown increasingly quieter and more distant. Summer was coming to a close, and autumn was taking its place. The others didn't feel the change as prominent as Stratus did. Sure, they felt room getting cooler due to the Air people subconsciously changing the temperature around them, but they hadn't taken too much notice as it was gradual and could easily go by unnoticed until one compared it to when the Air princess first arrived.

Pyra stared at the ceiling. She tossed a small piece of tungsten from her bed into the air, only to catch it again. This practice was how she spent her boredom. She had kept it when she started burning the bed because of this very practice.

Petunia sat on her bed studying a book Currentide had stolen from the library. When she questioned Currentide on this, Currentide, of course, said nothing in reply. Petunia felt bad, but she didn't know the exact placement of the book else she would have taken it back. Petunia kept it hidden in the dresser and only stared at its pages when there was not a captor near. She couldn't read the pages, but leaves were engraved on the front. It was filled with the foreign language as well as drawings of seeds and plants. It was still foreign to Petunia although the pictures reminded her of home.

Currentide, as usual, simply sat upon her bed peering into the minds of the other princesses. She'd done a lot more thinking after being kidnapped than she ever did at the Water Kingdom. There, she would at least communicate with people, but here it was lonelier because of her refusal to speak aloud. On the plus side, she was given a full glass of water every day for breathing purposes.

"So," said Pyra after a significant period of boredom, "what do you guys want to do?"

Petunia was too engrossed in her book to realize Pyra had spoken, and Cirrus was still being moody. Pyra sighed. This was going nowhere. She began playing with the fire on her bed. Even though her bed wasn't destroyed by the fire yet, to Pyra's surprise, she couldn't go anywhere without her footprints being visible to everyone because of the ashes on her feet. In the Fire Kingdom, volcanic ash is everywhere, and it's natural for feet to be dark. However, there weren't noticeable footprints there. Here everyone could see where she'd gone. She liked the soot, but the footprints brought about a large amount of frustration from her.

After maybe half an hour, an idea came to her. They could play catch, except using their different powers. They could deflect the piece of wood from the dresser to and from each other. A smile spread across Pyra's lips. She didn't particularly care for these other princesses, but if playing a game with them released her from the spell of boredom, she was all for it.

Pyra sliced a piece off the dresser, covered it in fire, and called it to her.

But who to throw it to first? Stratus's back was turned, so it wouldn't be too much fun since she wouldn't deflect it. Petunia was engrossed in that silly book, but Currentide was always just sitting there. Sitting there all the time and never speaking simply made Pyra a simmering level of mad. She thought Currentide could at least say a word or two every now and then. Pyra wanted to see how Currentide would react if Pyra threw the wood at her.

Pyra made her decision; Currentide it was. She didn't even say anything, but she merely threw the object at Currentide.

What happened next could not have been expected, not even Currentide expected it since she was too focused on Pyra's thoughts. Currentide had her sphere of water prepared to catch the wood, but the wood never landed in the water. Cirrus had built her own sphere of air and used that to grab the wood, only to throw it at Petunia.

Petunia, not quite expecting it, stopped the wood chunk at the last second. The piece was centimeters from her face. She slowly brought it down to her hand then wrapped her fingers around it. She said nothing and returned to her book.

Pyra sighed.

"Petunia," she said, but Petunia remained silent. "Petunia, we were only playing a game! You know, catch, but with our powers..." Petunia was still silent. "Ugh!"

Pyra rolled over. After a few minutes of silence, Stratus spoke up in a wispy voice.

"That was a game?" she asked.

"Uh, duh, Stratus."

"Oh. I thought I was just trying to beat you, guys."

"At what?"

Cirrus shrugged. Pyra made a *tch* sound and tried to find something else to do. The days where the princesses were locked in the room together were starting to take their toll. At first, they could find things to talk about and things to keep them from being killed by boredom. Now, everyone was becoming quieter, leaving Pyra feeling as if she was the only one in the room. She wished she was. She had to take action lest she lose her mind.

"Okay, that's it," she said.

She stood up and dragged the others three princesses off of their beds, making sure she had their undivided attention.

"All right, guys," she said with strange looks from the others. "Ugh, fine. *Girls.* Anyway, we'll have been here for a month within the next few days. I say it's time to escape, don't you think? We've all explored this building. We know practically every nook and cranny. Surely between the four of us, we can escape. Plus, we have powers that I don't think our captors have. We can easily overpower them. We can conquer them! We can escape!"

She realized how loud she was getting and quickly hushed.

"So tomorrow, whenever they allow us to roam the building, we escape. Today, however, we need to make a main plan of action, with several backup plans. Who's with me?"

Petunia was the only one to reply.

"I-I'm not very good at this rebelling you speak of," she said. "Wouldn't it be safer to stay here? Everything here is familiar, and our captors really aren't that bad. They're quite kind to us. Why should we leave? The Creator has a plan in mind, and we must allow Him to execute it."

One of Pyra's headaches was coming again. "So you're saying we should just stay put while our kingdoms and parents are all worried about us?"

"Well, not exactly, but…"

"What about the obstacle courses?" questioned Cirrus. "Natascha said I'll advance after this coming time. Can we at least stay long enough for me to find out where I'll be advancing?"

"No!" Pyra shouted. "If we wait any longer, we'll only be more intent on staying. We must leave tomorrow. Now, who's a good strategist?"

None of them answered her, since they weren't enthusiastic about leaving in the first place.

"Ugh! Do I have to do *everything* productive around here?"

She stormed back over to her fire and began formulating a plan of action for tomorrow. She hadn't ever done this much thinking back at the castle. Quickly she became homesick then began realizing the only way she could ever return was to escape from this wretched place of imprisonment.

The gears in her head began turning as a plan started to formulate. Yes, this had to come straight from the Creator for nothing else she had ever created was ever this—this perfect! He must want them to escape. Yes, it must be part of His plan for them. That was it; it had to be it.

She could hardly contain her joy. In fact, she couldn't. Her giggles were low and plentiful. Her grin had definitely shown through. The other girls had to stop what they were doing. Petunia was concerned for Pyra's health, and Stratus thought Pyra had gone demented.

"Fellow princesses," she said in the midst of her evil-sounding giggles. She also cocked her head to one side, eyes wide. "I have a plan. It is so perfect, you won't believe it. I believe it has come straight from the Creator." She looked toward the ceiling as if she could see through it and directly to the Creator. In the blink of an eye, her eyes darted back toward the others. "Are you ready for it?"

The others looked at each other, unsure whether they should listen or not. Slowly, they all agreed to listen.

"All right! First, we're going to need to distract the captors…"

Thus, she rattled off the entire plan, complete with backups and the like.

18

The Great Escape

When they awoke, the plan was to begin. Cirrus still lay on her bed when Petunia walked over to Pyra.

"Um," she said. "Last night, I made you some feet coverings. They're to cover up the ashes on your feet. I mean, if you don't want them, it's fine."

Pyra stared at Petunia for a while before she said anything. "That's genius, Petunia!"

It was said so loud Stratus turned over to see what had happened. While Pyra struggled with the leaf feet coverings, Petunia coaxed Cirrus out of her bed. Soon everyone was ready.

"Now," said Pyra before they left; the door was already ajar. "Do we all know the plan?"

The other princesses nodded.

"Then let's get out of here already!"

The girls left the room and proceeded to the nearest boarded up window. Pyra built up a ball of fire around her hand, then punched the decayed wood. It fell with satisfying thuds. Pyra turned to Stratus.

"Are you ready to do the honors?" she asked. Cirrus gave her a blank stare. "Um, Stratus?" Pyra sighed. "We talked about this last night, and you agreed to it. With your air powers, you're supposed to take us down to the ground."

Cirrus remained staring.

"Anytime would be great, Stratus."

Cirrus still did nothing.

"Anytime *today* preferably."

When Stratus continued to do nothing, Pyra began to lose it and started punching walls again. Petunia was confused, but Currentide knew exactly what was going on.

"It's fall, isn't it?" she said so quietly most may not have thought she had said anything at all, but the others didn't know her voice well. It was a surprise she had said anything at all.

Cirrus seemed to break from her trance for a moment.

"Why, yes," she replied. "It is. Today is the first day."

Currentide smiled, happy she was right. She waited minutes for the other two to catch on. It was Petunia who spoke it out loud.

"Oh!" she exclaimed. "That's right. The people of the Air Kingdom change attitudes according to the season. If it's fall, that means…that means it is the season where they become delicate. Now that we've mentioned it, she has been slowly becoming like this, hasn't she?"

"So you're saying," growled Pyra, "that she won't do her part of our plan because the seasons have changed?"

Petunia smiled, not yet seeing the problem. She laughed. "Yes, I guess so!"

Pyra punched the wall again. "Great, now we have to go to a more conspicuous backup plan."

Currentide crossed her arms and raised an eyebrow.

"So you're telling me that was your *least* conspicuous plan?" she said. The others stopped again. It was the beginning of the day, and Currentide had already spoken *twice?* This didn't seem right. "In that case, oh Great Creator, please help me with these more obvious plans. I fear our recapture."

"You know," Petunia piped up again, "if we wait until winter Cirrus might be in a better shape then. Oh wait… maybe not. I think the Air people become mean in the winter. Well, we could wait until spring! She'll be really happy and joyful at that point in time!"

"I am not waiting until spring to escape!" shouted Pyra.

"Don't be too loud now," Currentide said. "Our captors might hear you."

"I liked you better when you didn't talk."

"I actually despise talking, but alas, it's the only way to communicate to you who are from other kingdoms."

"What do you mean?"

"Oh, nothing!"

Pyra growled. "Let's just continue on with the first backup plan."

They all followed Pyra down the two flights of stairs and to the first floor.

"Ooh!" said Currentide. "We're on the first floor! How conspicuous!"

Pyra ignored her. The group's eyes went wide at the sight of Natascha walking toward them and looking at some object in her hand. They couldn't be found out, not now. The plan was almost complete.

"Quick!" said Pyra. "Hide!"

They each went into a separate cubicle as fast as they could. Albeit, Stratus was dragged and pushed into one by Petunia who apologized immediately afterward. They all breathed as silent and slow as they could muster. They heard Natascha's heels clicking the hard floor. The sound only got louder and louder as she came closer and closer. Their hearts (save Cirrus) were beating hard and fast. The princesses wouldn't have been surprised if Natascha could hear the heartbeats. Would they be caught before they could even sniff the smell of freedom?

Natascha's heels stopped. The princesses weren't sure what that meant, but Stratus could easily see Natascha's feet. She stared at them curiously, thinking her feet coverings were strange. Then she cursed herself for not being as good or beautiful as the others. She shouldn't have been wondering about the strange things upon Natascha's feet. The others were all scared of being found out. She needed to be more like them, but she couldn't.

"Hello?" Natascha ventured.

None of the girls answered and hardly breathed, lest they wanted Natascha to know where they were. Natascha sighed.

"Look, I know you're in here. There's no use hiding."

Petunia started to rise when Currentide used her mind to force Petunia to become still once again. Natascha had noticed the brief movement but had merely darted her eyes toward it. She looked straight at Petunia's hiding place now.

They remained still as even more minutes passed. Eventually, Natascha got tired of standing around and pulled each one of them up and out of their hiding place. Pyra and Currentide prepared separate attacks so they could escape. Two were better than one, right? Surely they could overpower her. Just as they were about to attack, Natascha shocked their wristbands.

"Now," she questioned, "why were the four of you hiding and then two of you about to attack me?"

Petunia began crying.

"I'm so sorry!" she wailed. "I tried to stop them, but… but—I'm sorry!"

She wailed even louder. Natascha gave her a confused glance.

"Um, are you saying you tried to stop them just now?"

"What?" Petunia managed to ask.

"Yes!" Pyra jumped in. "Currentide and I *were* trying to attack you, and Petunia tried to stop us, but you shocked us before she could intervene."

Natascha nodded.

"But," she said, "that still doesn't explain why you were hiding from me on your exploration day."

"Oh that…" Pyra said. "Well…we were playing hide-and-seek! Right, guys?"

Currentide nodded, Petunia was still crying, and Stratus wasn't paying attention for she was too absorbed in internally putting herself down. Natascha simply shook her head.

"Whatever, Princesses. Just don't get into trouble, all right?"

With a shake of her head, she turned around and the clicking of the heels continued. Pyra and Currentide waited to sigh until Natascha was out of earshot. They waited a few minutes for Petunia to compose herself, but after the few minutes, she might have been crying even harder. They weren't certain. Pyra groaned and took matters into her own hands.

She took the two strides to Petunia. Then, Pyra grabbed Petunia's shoulders and shook—hard.

"Get a hold of yourself!" she nearly screamed. Frightened, Petunia stopped. Pyra stopped and crossed her arms. "You guys—girls… If we're going to do this, it needs to be now or never. If we keep waiting, who knows when the next opportunity will arise—"

"Well," interrupted Currentide with a smirk, "the Creator knows, and we'll have a chance every week on the exploration day."

Pyra glared at her and continued on. "So we need to seize this chance and go before it's too late!"

Petunia and Currentide, despite her own comment, were pumped by Pyra's inspirational speech. They were ready to escape because Pyra was right, it might as well be now or never. So the princesses, dragging Cirrus behind, went to a window. Currentide nodded at Pyra who punched it with fire again, just like the last one.

Pyra, after making sure the coast was clear inside and outside (what she could see at least), stepped out of their place of imprisonment. She motioned the others to follow. Petunia went out and helped Stratus go through. Currentide checked once more inside then followed the others. She couldn't see them but could feel their minds' presences close by.

At the back of the building, she chose to head to her right. There was a small indention on the wall, but if one was to press her body against it, she would not be seen by the window they escaped from. Her fellow princesses, however, were not there. Consequently Currrentide continued on her fortuitous way.

Around the next corner, she found the other princesses. She noticed why they must have chosen to remain here until Currentide joined them. It really was intelligent of them to pick it: it was further from the window they escaped from, and there were no other windows in case someone happened to look out and see glimpses of the escapees.

They walked further away from captivity. Cirrus would remember the ground, for her eyes were downcast, and whatever she saw out of her peripheral vision, but the other girls didn't notice it too terribly much. There were few trees in sight, and the grass was a dull color. All plants were sad little dead things. The air was thick; although the residents made a futile attempt to help what environment was left. The princesses were finding it a challenge to breathe. Buildings were past the horizon, the start of a town. There was a strange sound far off in the distance to the right—in front of the building they were kept in. It was kind of like a whoosh over and over combined with an odd whirring noise. There wasn't water nearby on the land, but much lay underneath in pipes.

Currentide high-fived the others, including Stratus who simply had her hand out. Petunia quietly cheered, but Pyra spoke up.

"We can't cheer just yet, girls! We're not home free yet! We still need to leave the outskirts of this building. Hurry!" She began sprinting, and the others followed. "Right now, they can still—"

Pyra stopped dead in her tracks. The others passed her. They were many steps ahead before they noticed her absence. It was Currentide who picked it up first via mind waves. She noticed an immediate change in Pyra's mind. She, too, stopped abruptly. She looked back at Pyra for she could see nothing in Pyra's mind.

The other two noticed half of their group wasn't running with them, although Cirrus's was more of a fast walk or slow jog.

"Pyra?" Petunia ventured.

No one could see inside Pyra's mind for she was getting a vision. This hadn't happened in such a long time. Pyra was beginning to think that maybe she couldn't receive visions like the others in the Fire Kingdom could.

In her vision, she saw the four princesses. That was a very clear image. They weren't in the room they had been residing in, but another. There was also another person, a girl? The other person was very blurry. Pyra couldn't quite make out the person's features. The person also emanated the feeling of being…different. Pyra couldn't quite place it.

At first, she wondered if it had to do with the skin. The other four's skin seemed bright compared to this other person.

Well, Pyra thought in her vision while looking at her own skin, *I mean, I'm* orange. *Compared to the other princesses I'm pretty weird, right?*

The whole image started to go fuzzy. Pyra got the feeling this wasn't supposed to happen.

"Creator!" She tried to cry out, but her voice made no sound. "Creator, help me! What's going on?"

Everything was shaking. Slowly the image was going out of focus. She tried to run toward it, but it was as if no matter how fast or hard she ran forward, the image continued to leave her. It finally faded into oblivion.

Pyra stomped her foot, but it didn't hit solid ground. Before she knew it, she was falling, falling, falling...

Falling.

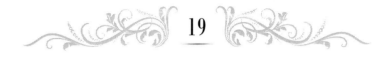

19

A Change

All the girls awoke with a throbbing headache. The moment Pyra awoke, since she had slept the longest, the door opened, and Natascha walked in. Her face looked very stern. She had that strange object in her hand again.

"My partner is here to speak with you. Get up."

"Can it wait until my head *doesn't* feel like it's going to explode?" asked Pyra with an obvious strain on her face. "Better yet, he could come in here for once rather than hiding in front of that stupid light. It's not like we've never seen him before."

Natascha's facial expression did not change during this. "You have five minutes before we force you to come out."

After saying this, Natascha left. The princesses groaned. Petunia tried to go, but her headache prevented her from moving too much. Currentide tried as well, but it made her mind weaker and thus harder to read the others' minds. She couldn't handle not reading their minds, but her head hurt so badly. The pain simply intensified Stratus's hatred of herself. If she couldn't even try to overcome this headache then how could she manage to do anything else in life? She'd never be as good as the others who obviously were trying to fight it. Cirrus was a coward to not even attempt it. Pyra wanted to scream at the pain. She toyed with the idea of punching the wall again, wondering if the pain would transfer over or if she would simply be in even more pain.

"Can we just not go out there?" questioned Pyra.

"But they want us to," Petunia protested. "What if... what if we obey them? Maybe they'll simply let us free?"

"Oh, yes. Kidnappers will simply let those they just kidnapped free, simply because they were good little captives. That will most definitely happen."

Petunia looked down. Her heart wanted to believe Pyra wasn't being sarcastic, but her wisdom instincts knew better. Before the girls knew it, Natascha was back at the door. None of them had stepped off their beds. They didn't think Natascha would be as furious as she was.

"This rebellion is out of hand!" she yelled. "If you don't get out of those beds within the next two seconds, pain like no other you have ever felt will come upon you!"

Scared out of their wits, the princesses quickly jumped out of the beds, which was a very bad idea where their headaches were concerned. They followed Natascha to the light behind the other captor once again. He spoke very,

very quietly. The girls were forced to strain in order to hear him.

"How dare you try and escape.... We have provided you with all of your needs, and this is how you repay us? Yes, we did kidnap you four, and I guess that might be a good reason to escape...but nonetheless!

"If you princesses try this again, there won't be as much grace as there is this time. There will be no mercy next time. You will be begging for us to return to previous punishments you've received.

"Don't worry, you will still be punished for this attempt, it just won't be as severely as the next time it happens. Keep that in mind."

He leaned back in his chair and pressed his fingertips against each other. A wicked smile spread across his lips.

"Now, today you will be doing the obstacle courses, but you won't be doing the ones you're used to doing. Today, we'd like to take the Air princess to the obstacle course of earth and the Water princess to the obstacle course of air. Also, you will be going every other day to these courses. There is no longer a day for exploration. In place of that day there is a day of rest. This means you will be going three times a week to an obstacle course. Natascha, take those of whom we do not require a service to their room."

Natascha obeyed wordlessly.

Once they were inside the vehicle, the kidnappers gave the two princesses shots. Quickly, the two girls were fast asleep. The male captor drove to their first destination: the obstacle course of air. Natascha startled him slightly by speaking.

"Sorry," she apologized. "I just wanted to make sure you knew you were taking Princess Currentide and I was dealing with Princess Cirrus or Stratus or whatever her name is."

"I knew that," he said shortly.

Natascha said no more in the duration of the ride.

"Do you understand?"

"I think so," Currentide replied. "Just to refresh my memory, in a few minutes I'm supposed to jump out of this flying vehicle and land on the course?"

"Yes," he said. "Oh, here."

He handed her goggles, which she put on.

"In a few seconds, you must jump. If you don't, everything will be messed up, and we'll have to fly around once more. I have to take care of something real fast."

He went to the cockpit to give instructions. Currentide took deep breaths: breathing in…then out. She had to psyche her mind out in order to do this. Being up this high was completely unnatural. She kept fearing she was about to fall out of this helicopter, so she gripped tightly onto whatever she could to stabilize herself.

Her captor came back.

"Are you ready?"

She nodded. It was now or never.

"Good," he replied. "Because you need to jump in three…two…one!"

Princess Currentide jumped and spread her arms out. This felt completely wrong; it sent shivers throughout her body. No, this wasn't right. It could never be right.

Her stomach slammed onto a pole-like object. She opened her eyes and noticed it was a hoop. She clutched for dear life. Adjusting herself, she looked and saw more hoops. Her eyes widened. What kind of course was this?

She tried to reach up to the next hoop, but the one she was on was slowly sinking. She ever so slowly stood on the hoop then jumped off. Her fingertips brushed the hoop, and the next thing she knew, she was falling.

The hoop she was previously on was rising back to its original place. She grabbed for it and managed to get a grip on it. She tried to quickly climb back to the top to jump off again. After she jumped, she managed to get a grip on the next hoop; she continued to use the same tactic on the rest of the hoops. When she jumped off and onto the platform, she breathed a sigh of relief. There was a bucket of water which Currentide used to add to her current supply on her gills.

Currentide walked across the platform, glad to be on something solid again. When she reached the other edge, she looked around. There was another platform on up ahead, but Currentide couldn't cross it by merely jumping. She looked down. Her eyes betrayed her for what she perceived to be a speck in the clouds, was a spring to bounce her toward the next platform. She looked over at her captor who stood on the platform as well. She looked back down and jumped.

As she fell, she noticed the speck gradually getting larger. She veered away from it, attempting to use some of her water to propel her closer to the ground. Sadly, it was still very far away. She continued to fall for minutes more as her captor caught up, but she didn't see him getting closer.

The wind whipped her face until he caught her and took her back to the helicopter. Currentide beat him and tried to push herself out of his grip but to no avail.

"Unhand me!" she screeched.

"If you understand, just nod or say yes or something!" Natascha ended up yelling at the Air princess.

Cirrus flinched. Why was this woman yelling at her? Had she done something wrong? Of course she had. Why did she even need to ask? Stratus was always being bad, that's why people didn't like her.

Cirrus looked off into the distance, her mind far away from Natascha. Natascha sighed.

"Look," she continued. "The course stands before you. You need to do it. You cannot use your powers. This is the last time I'm going to tell you. Got it?"

Stratus cowered away and pointed to the course in front of her, finally noticing its presence. Natascha nodded and began massaging her forehead. Cirrus slowly floated off the tree and toward the obstacle course. It was an uphill climb with a rope attached. She grabbed the rope and held it lightly in her hands, gazing at it. It appeared to be intricately woven and caught Stratus's eye. She wished she could make something as interesting as this, but she didn't have that kind of courage. She couldn't ever make something great. She was worthless and had nothing good to add to anyone's life.

"You're supposed to climb up, using the rope for support," Natascha interrupted.

Cirrus looked back at the rope. Was that what she was supposed to do? Of course, she was an idiot, wasn't she? A good-for-nothing who couldn't figure anything out on her own. She wished she could do something on her own for once.

She looked back up at the climb. She reached for a higher spot on the rope, then for another. She fell to the ground from not moving her feet. The fall made her bum and clothing dirty. She was in physical pain, but it was nothing compared to the emotional weight she'd placed upon herself. As she sat on the ground, she hung her head once more. She couldn't even get past the first obstacle that was laid out before her. How could she even hope to eventually complete the entire course?

Cirrus looked back and saw Natascha. She was in the same spot from earlier, and her arms were crossed.

"Well, are you going to continue on?" she prompted.

Stratus looked back at the first obstacle. Could she get past this first feat, which would surely lead to many more? She stood up, grabbed the rope once more, and began ascending once again. Her grip was tighter, but she hardly noticed. She moved her feet this time as well, but she didn't notice that either. All she knew was she wanted to be done with everything unfamiliar so she could go back home where she belonged. Here, there was nothing for her.

When she finally reached the top, she let go of the rope and floated onward. She proceeded to receive a great shock. The wooden circle dug into her back, causing Cirrus to arch a little. She arched too much and fell to the ground.

Her body could not handle such a shock. It had immediately gone limp once it spread throughout her limbs. She fell unconscious as well. As she lay on the ground, her last thoughts before fading away were, *If only I was better... then I wouldn't have fallen. The Creator does not smile upon me, does He? He doesn't want me, I can feel it. I shouldn't even be alive. I should have died, not her...*

Natascha walked over to Cirrus, sighed, and scooped her up. Natascha carried Stratus's limp body to the car. What was she, Natascha, going to do if Cirrus kept this up? It took her way too long to finish the first obstacle. She couldn't keep doing this if Stratus was going to do this every time. She just might trade princesses with her partner.

With those thoughts in mind, she drove back to the place of imprisonment.

20

An Attempt to Return to an Old Tradition

The Earth and Fire princesses awoke to being yanked off of their beds the next morning.

"Hey, watch it!" Pyra retaliated as she yanked her arm away from her captors. "This body is priceless. If you return me back to my parents with injuries who knows how angry they'll get?"

Pyra shivered once the frozen floor made contact with her feet. All the while Petunia was wondering what was in store for them today. She thought about how doing a different element's obstacle course was a suitable punishment for trying to escape. It seemed right for them to be reprimanded for their action; it was only fair. Petunia decided she would try her best at the obstacle course today, no matter which element it was in.

Once the princesses were in the vehicle bound and blindfolded, their captors began explaining a few things.

"So," said Natascha as her partner drove, "Princess Pyra will be attending the obstacle course of water today, and Princess Petunia will be going to the obstacle course of fire. Princess Pyra will be dropped off at hers first."

Natascha injected something into the princesses' arms. They went unconscious.

Pyra awoke to heat upon her skin. It felt most wonderful to finally be warm. She wanted to soak in this all day. She breathed in and out. There was a salty tang to the air, but she didn't mind.

"Oh, good," a voice said. "You're up."

Pyra opened her eyes to see Natascha standing over her, hands on hips.

"Oh, great," Pyra said. "*You're* still here."

Natascha raised an eyebrow. "Did you think I had left?"

"I'm going to be honest here and say I had hoped you had. Sadly the Creator has not answered my prayer for you to die in the bitter cold."

Natascha pursed her lips and continued on.

"The obstacle course is underwater. I'll give you an air tank, so you can breathe. We can't have you dying on us, now can we?"

Pyra stood up and brushed the sand off her body. She was given a wet suit to put on along with fins to go over her feet. Natascha then handed her a cylinder with tubes spreading from it. She instructed Pyra on how to put it on and eventually sighed and helped her. Pyra noticed Natascha was wearing one as well. Natascha also had a heavy vest, which Pyra needed to put on as well.

Natascha then proceeded to grab Pyra's wrist and jump into the water. Pyra, not having put the mouthpiece on her mouth, began sputtering under the water. Natascha was then forced to bring Pyra above the water.

"You have to wear your mouthpiece!" Natascha instructed. "Otherwise you'll swallow the water and die. You and I don't breathe like Currentide and therefore must wear these in order for us to be under as long as required for the obstacle course. Also, try to breathe through your mouth and not your nose."

Pyra obeyed, put the mouthpiece in her mouth, adjusted her goggles then went back underwater. It took her a few minutes to only breathe through her mouth and not through her nose. She attempted to go toward strands of ropes, which lay below her, but she didn't know how to swim. This became a very difficult task to undertake.

Her body tended to go float upward without Pyra's asking. She tried many desperate attempts to go toward the rope. Walking proved to be a failure as did flailing one's limbs as did flapping like a bird as well as imitating the nearby fish. Pyra found the water to be cold, and she wasn't growing accustomed to it.

Natascha wished they could just call it a day already since Pyra obviously wasn't going to figure out how to swim on her own, but Natascha was required to wait a little longer. The kidnappers had agreed to not tell their captives how to complete the obstacle courses. For Pyra, this involved teaching her how to swim.

Slowly, Pyra began to watch Natascha and attempted to copy her. This plan proved to be somewhat helpful, but the movements were too complicated for Pyra. It would have worked had Natascha not been on one of the best swim teams years ago. By Pyra's copying, she simply ended up doing even more flailing. Pyra wanted to scream in anger at her evil captors.

In fact, she did.

"You! You! You...you..."

This was all she managed while her mouthpiece fell out. Water had entered her esophagus, causing her to not breathe. Natascha swooped down toward Pyra's falling body. She carried Pyra's heavy figure to the surface and the beach. Natascha took off her goggles and mouthpiece.

Natascha felt for a pulse then pressed on Pyra's diaphragm. She patted Pyra's cheeks in the hope Pyra would simply cough up the water. When she didn't awake, Natascha resorted to her package of pills.

Looking through them, she decided on one that caused the consumer to throw up the water from inside. It was risky and required immediate water after the initial effect, but Natascha hoped it would work. She needed it to, because otherwise…

She pressed it into Pyra's mouth then grabbed the jug of water and brought it to her patient. When she came back, the pill had already kicked in. Natascha took the cap off the jug and handed it to Pyra. Pyra refused it. Natascha was worried.

"If you don't drink it, your body will surely die from dehydration!" she retaliated.

Pyra gave her a look that said, *Are you* serious?

"You're *so* dumb," she said. "If I drink it, I'll die. You do realize I come from the *Fire* Kingdom, right?"

With that, she stood back up. Natascha yanked her back down by the ankle then knocked her unconscious by whacking her on the head. Natascha dragged Pyra's body to the boat, started the engine, then drove away from the island and back to shore.

"Excuse me, but you want me to do what *exactly*?" Petunia questioned.

"I just need you complete the obstacle course," the male captor replied. "The fire is and will continue to be lit throughout the entire course.

"Are you s-sure I won't die?"

"Well, no promises, but you shouldn't under my watch."

She took deep breaths. This was a rightful punishment. She did try to escape. Petunia looked up to the sky and prayed to the Creator. She prayed for strength to overcome this obstacle course if that was His will. She barely heard the captor say she may begin whenever she was ready.

Well, it was now or never. Quickly, she passed the first wall of fire and looked at her first obstacle. There were circular objects on the ground with holes in them the rough size of a foot. Petunia could only figure she must step one foot at a time into each object. She did this at a fast pace, trying her best not to get burned by the surrounding fire.

She lightly stepped out and looked at the next obstacle which lay before her. There were steep stairs; she ascended them carefully. When she reached the top, she rejoiced. The beginning was over, and now she felt as if she could conquer the rest of the course. No! She mustn't judge the rest of the course too quickly!

She saw the next obstacle in which jumps were involved. Petunia's heart rate went up a little. The obstacle required her to jump toward a pole then to another and another. She leaned as far as she dared, leading into the jump. She stumbled as she grabbed the pole. Her body started slipping. She reached for the next pole, but there was no way to do it without jumping. Petunia braced herself and jumped. She luckily reached the pole and was holding on tightly once again.

She continued jumping from pole to pole until she reached the tenth one. Petunia jumped onto a platform, taking a breather. Her next obstacle in this course was a simple downhill slope, but with the addition of spikes poking in and out.

At first, Petunia tried shuffling her feet around the spikes for she could see the holes and recognized a pattern. When this proved to not work and she fell down, she simply tried to avoid the spikes at all costs. She rolled down the slope accidentally timing it right so that she wasn't too seriously injured.

She quickly stood up and looked to the heavens.

Dearest Creator, I know I shouldn't question You, but why are You putting me through this? What is Your plan?

She looked at her next obstacle and faced it head on. She quickly climbed up the ladder until she was on a platform large enough to only hold her feet. A silver mesh of rope stretched across onto another small platform. She reached for the mesh and quickly situated her footing. She was going across smoothly, sweat dripping from her brow like she'd just gotten out of a pool of water.

One of her hands slipped. Her foot followed simultaneously. She couldn't grab ahold of the mesh again for her hands were too sweaty. Her right hand quickly fell also. The mesh was too unstable for her to keep her balance; thus, she fell to the ground.

∽⟨∞⟩∽

"You're back. What's the news?"

"Um, well, Your Majesty, we've searched the whole kingdom like you asked, but…um, have yet to find any signs of the princess."

The rulers banged their fists against their thrones.

"What is the meaning of this!?" The servant said nothing in reply. "What are you doing just kneeling there? Go take your team and search it again!"

"Y-yes, Your Highnesses," the servant mumbled and left quickly.

The anger boiled in the queen and king. The queen spoke. "We've hired the best detectives and search parties, and none of them have found the heir to our throne. Why can losing a princess be this easy? Why can't we find her?"

The other ruler had his head in his hands.

"I don't know. That's the problem. We know nothing that has happened. We don't know who or why, but only a brief idea of when. This is why we can't even think about it without getting lost at the thought of it. It's never occurred before, so we're not sure what to make of it."

The rulers proceeded to sit in silence. While this was happening, the Earth leaders, Queen Chikyū and King Jigu, were discussing almost the same matter.

"Chikyū," said Jigu, "an idea is beginning to brew in my head, but I'm not sure if it will work or not."

"Well, voice your thoughts, and we shall discuss it and see," Chikyū replied.

"All four of the princesses disappearing simultaneously seems to be too precise and odd to be a coincidence. If this is the case, then I'm wondering if all of the rulers should work together. If we all searched for them, surely we would find them eventually?"

"Well," Chikyū replied, "I'm not sure the others would agree to this proposal. The Air Kingdom is at their worst right now, the Fire Kingdom still thinks we did it, and the Water Kingdom…I don't even know what they'll say.

"However, I find your idea to be wise overall and would work if the other kingdoms were more open. I'm not saying they're not perfect in the way the Creator made them. I'm saying it's not easy."

Jigu placed his hand over Chikyū's. He smiled at her and said, "I know."

Chikyū stood up.

"Your idea is worth a try, however. We shall start writing the letters today. If even one other kingdom agrees then maybe we'll both be one step closer to finding our daughters."

With that, the two rulers started the process of letter writing.

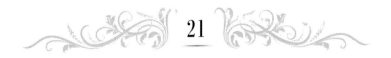

21

Secrets

By the time the week was over, all four princesses had attempted every obstacle course and had also completed none of them. The day of rest had passed, and today Petunia and Cirrus were gone doing obstacle courses once again. This left Currentide and Pyra by themselves in the room.

Once Pyra awoke, she began thinking, mainly about Currentide. Currentide keyed in as usual. After a half hour or so of thinking, Pyra came to a decision, which she voiced.

"All those times I've felt that 'other presence' that's woken me up… It's been you, hasn't it? Of course, I can't prove it, but I know. Oh, I know. And all I can wonder is if you've been doing it to the others. Petunia wouldn't know the difference, and I bet Stratus would fall apart if she found out.

"Now, the big question is when I should break the news to them that you've been reading our minds this whole time. Should I do it tonight when they get back and are physically exhausted and can't think straight? Or should I wait until the next resting day where we'll be locked in a room together *all day* long? Or maybe—"

"STOP!" Currentide screamed and placed her hands to her ears, a practice she rarely did. Pyra was taken aback, but smiled nonetheless.

"Oh?" Pyra said as if talking to a baby. "Does little Currentide not like it when ol' evil Pyra figures things out? Is that a problem for you? Because this isn't even the worst I can do. I could also—"

"Just shut up," Currentide growled. She then thought back to what Pyra said earlier and decided to use Pyra's words against her. Currentide straightened once more. "You can't prove it; you said it yourself. Even if you do, the others can't possibly believe you. You're always being mean to them. What makes you think they'll believe this nonsense? I'm simply quiet most of the time. They can't have anything against me."

Pyra pointed accusingly.

"Oh!" she said. "But since you're quiet most of the time you could be reading our minds rather than talking!"

"True, but who says I'm not reading your mind whilst we're conversing right now?"

These words stopped Pyra. Now she had to check her mind to see if what Currentide said was true. Was she reading her mind? She didn't feel a weird presence, but she'd only recognized it a few times before anyway. Pyra began her next words slowly and carefully.

"I bet you're not reading it now, because I've accused you. This way I can't say that you are because you're not doing it, but that doesn't mean you haven't done it before."

Currentide's arms were crossed now. "Do *you* even know what you're saying?"

Pyra tried to tone down her anger.

"Look," she said, "I know what I've felt, okay? I've never felt it before. It makes the most sense for you to be doing it, unless the captors are just *really* good at playing dumb, which I doubt."

"And who says it's not the captors?"

"I do. You also do realize that on our first day here we recited the Creation story, and in that, we discussed the Water Kingdom being able to read minds, right? I figured you, of all people, should know that since, you know, you're from the Water Kingdom and all."

Currentide just closed her eyes and pretended Pyra wasn't there. This was very hard since Currentide could easily feel Pyra's mind blatantly screaming at her. Oh, it was making her mad, so very, very mad. Pyra was really just sending random thoughts and simple sentences, but she was yelling them in the hope Currentide could easily hear her. For Currentide, it really just felt like someone was speaking at the top of her lungs right in her ear. Currentide couldn't take it anymore. She spoke in the wrong way without meaning to.

Shut up already! I can hear you perfectly fine when you talk to me normally. A whisper is just as easy!

"Yes!" Pyra said whilst pulling her fist down. She then pointed to Currentide. "I knew it! I knew it! You can read minds! Speaking of which, what all *can* you do?"

Currentide sighed inwardly as she was used to doing. She then shifted a little uncomfortably.

Well, this is weird to explain how the mind works to someone who's never known whilst I've been accustomed to it my whole life. I guess... This is just weird.

Okay, um, I can send you messages—didn't know I could do that before—but I'm not sure if you can send them back. I think you can think your thoughts, and I can read your mind and know what you thought. In the Water Kingdom we can block our minds from reading each other's thoughts. If you're from the Water Kingdom and I don't want you to read my thoughts, then I should build up a good mind block.

"Can't you do anything interesting?" Pyra said aloud. "I mean, besides finding out some cool, deep, dark secrets, can you do anything useful?"

If you become good at mind reading, like me and my parents, you can control the thoughts of others.

"Well, why didn't you start off with that?! Do you know what this means? We can totally escape! It's perfect! You can just make our captors *want* to let us go! We're home-free!"

It doesn't exactly work like that... When you control someone else's mind, you simply plant the seed. The person doesn't even have to do it, because it's his or her choice. It all depends on how susceptible the person is and how good his or her mind block is.

"Our captors don't have a mind block, though, do they? Shouldn't only those in the Water Kingdom be able to do it well?"

That's the problem. I can feel your mind and Petunia's mind and Cirrus's mind, but...

Currentide was too scared to admit it. It had never happened before. She refused to tell someone, especially someone from another kingdom. If there was anyone from the Water Kingdom here, then maybe they could figure it out together. Someone from another kingdom couldn't even begin to help her figure it out.

"But what?" Pyra prompted.

Currentide shook her head. No, she wouldn't tell someone else. It felt wrong.

Pyra placed her hands on her hips. "Currentide, I can't help you if you don't tell me what it is."

You couldn't help me even if I told you...

Pyra was taken aback. She wasn't good with girly emotional stuff. Not many people in the Fire Kingdom got sad; they experienced anger and laughter more than anything else. Pyra wasn't sure how she was supposed to deal with Currentide right now.

"Um…well, maybe…if you tell me I could…I can… It will help you because…you'll have told someone and… maybe by talking it out you can…?"

Pyra knew her feeble attempt hadn't worked. She brought her knees up to her chest and wrapped her arms around them, holding one wrist. The two sat in silence for a long time, both absorbed in their thoughts. Currentide was debating whether to tell Pyra or not, and Pyra was trying to entertain herself whilst figuring out how to get Currentide to tell her.

"I…" said Currentide, cutting through the apathy. Pyra moved her head to look at her Water Kingdom acquaintance. "I can't read our captors' minds."

Pyra said nothing. Currentide continued.

"Whenever I try, it's as if there wasn't a person there at all. I feel nothing coming from them. A mind block would feel different. With them I feel—there's nothing *to* feel."

She shivered. Pyra stared at the ground, finally understanding. Yes, if Currentide could control the minds of their captors, then by now she would have, and they would have left on day one.

You won't tell the other two, right?

"About what?" Pyra whispered.

About how I've been reading all three of your minds. If Stratus found out, it would break her heart, and Petunia would be fine, but…I don't want more people to know than necessary.

"Don't we all technically already know?"

Yes, but you're not wary of it. You don't think, "Oh, Currentide's probably reading my thoughts right now, isn't she?" *No, you girls don't pay attention to it like that, and I'd rather it stay the way it is.*

"Girl, I got you! I won't tell the others that you've been reading our minds all this time!"

Sh!

Pyra laughed at Currentide. Oh, the joys of watching people worry over nothing when Pyra caused it. The girls continued about their day and went to sleep earlier than they would have in their respective kingdoms since they had obstacle courses to do the next day. This was part of the tiresome work being kidnapped required. Woe to them.

22

All Alone

The rest of the week went by as usual. The princesses did obstacle courses, and Pyra purposely slipped snippets about mind reading. Currentide was starting to get upset. If she kept it up, Currentide was going to give Pyra a piece of her mind and show her not to mess with those from the Water Kingdom, especially if that person was the princess.

The other two didn't notice too much of a difference. Stratus was still wallowing in self-pity. Petunia was polite and kind as always. She would still stare at the pages of the book whenever she could and learn nothing because of her ignorance of the language.

It was the day of rest and the four princesses were sleeping peacefully in their beds when the door opened and a loud noise resounded.

"Rise and shine, Princesses, we're changing it up today!"

Petunia rose without struggle for she was an early riser anyway. Cirrus and Currentide slowly arose. Pyra simply moaned in her bed and covered her face, refusing to get up. Natascha sighed and yanked Pyra out of bed while the others rubbed their eyes and stood up.

"Follow me, Princesses. You're taking this trip all at the same time."

"Wow," Pyra said. "This is like an epiphany for you guys! Are you going to knock us all out?"

Natascha stopped and gave her a perplexed look.

"Why wouldn't we knock you out? We don't usually change protocol, and when we do, it's for the better."

Natascha continued walking, and the others followed her once more. Once they all got into the same vehicle (although now the inside was much bigger, allowing the girls to sit and still not touch each other) the usual routine of bound limbs, a blindfold, and being knocked out began. Most of the time, they were good captives to their kidnappers.

They awoke in a very large room consisting of a giant fish tank, another obstacle course covered with vines, floating platforms, and rings of fire. Each of these was stationed the same way as the beds in the princesses room were. The tank was in the back right corner; the vine-covered obstacle course was across from it in the back left corner. The platforms were on the left as the princesses looked at the room, the rings on their right.

The other captor appeared along with Natascha and began speaking.

"Oh, good, you're up. As you can see, we've devised a place for you to practice the obstacle courses. I think of it as a type of training ground. This is where you girls can help each other in areas that need be taught and not figured out on your own. You may only use your powers only if you are in your element. Otherwise, you will be shocked. Is this understood?"

All four princesses nodded.

"Good," said Natascha. "You have until five this evening to practice and train. You may begin."

Of course, all four of the princesses immediately went to their respective elements so they could use their powers without being shocked. It seemed the most wonderful thing that had ever happened. Just as they were all about to enter their sections, Natascha spoke up.

"Oh, and did we forget to mention that there must always be at least two"—here, she lifted up her index and middle fingers—"of you at a section? We aren't allowing you to go by yourselves now."

Pyra became very angry.

"Oh, yeah?" she challenged. "And what will happen if don't listen to you?"

"You'll be isolated from the others and basically have contact with no one else."

"Oh, you think that, but—"

Currentide stopped Pyra from speaking via her mind. She saw Pyra was about to ruin Currentide's secret and stopped her before it was too late. She desperately wanted no one else to know until it was absolutely necessary.

"But what?" Natascha challenged back.

"But..." Pyra had lost her train of thought. Currentide gave her an idea, which Pyra took. "But I talk to myself a lot, so I won't ever be alone."

Natascha shook her head and mumbled something about stupid, crazy princesses.

The princesses looked at each other.

"I'll go with someone to their area," Petunia offered. "Currentide, is it okay if I go with you? I need to work on my swimming, but only if you're willing to teach me."

Currentide sent a message to Pyra. They'd been practicing how to communicate with their minds. Pyra couldn't send messages, but she could think them, and Currentide would still receive them. They'd grown really close after the past week, practically shunning the other two.

Is it all right for me to teach Petunia? I mean, we all have things to work on...

Pyra thought her reply. *We can meet up later, there's plenty of time. Maybe we can discuss escape plans?*

Again?

Pyra smiled and walked over to Cirrus and grabbed her arm.

"Okay," said Pyra, "you're coming with me into the fire today. I'll teach you how to not die."

Stratus said nothing in reply.

After a while, Pyra was fed up with Cirrus for doing nothing besides cowering away. Pyra ended up storming away, forced to drag Stratus behind her so she herself wouldn't get shocked. In the other corner, Petunia and Currentide had a good lesson on swimming. Then, Pyra continued to storm all the way to the tank. She put the gear on and jumped in. She flailed her way over toward Currentide and Petunia who were near the top, but a foot or two under.

"You're getting it," Currentide said. "Let's try it again. Oh, hello, Pyra."

I'm going to kill her, Pyra thought whilst shivering. *I'm going to kill her. She can't do anything, Currentide!*

Currentide simply cocked her head. She was still watching Petunia perform the exercise. Once she came back, Currentide spoke once again.

"Hey, you're improving! I think I'm going to teach Pyra next. You can stay, I don't mind teaching both of you, but I think Pyra would rather do it alone." Currentide covered her hand as she whispered the next sentence in Petunia's ear, "She doesn't like people watching her bad swimming."

Petunia nodded, waved good-bye, and swam toward the platform where she would take off her gear then begin descending the ladder. Once she reached the ground floor again, she saw Stratus staring at something from afar. Happily, Petunia walked over to her.

"Hello, Cirrus!" she said in a cheerful voice. "Princess Pyra is having a swimming lesson from Princess Currentide. Would you like to teach me something about air, or do you want me to teach you something about Earth? I can do either, it's all up to you. Oh, by the way, you look gorgeous today! In fact, you're probably one of the prettier ones out of the four of us! You're also really talented, and it would be amazing if you could show your dazzling smiles more often!"

Stratus slowly cocked her head at the Earth princess. Why was she being so nice to her? Cirrus was worthless and shouldn't even be talking to nice people. She should go see if Pyra would mind her tagging along on the swimming lesson, so Stratus could take her rightful place of being yelled at once more. Yes, she might just go do that.

But wait. She shouldn't be rude to Petunia either.

"Thank you," she found her mouth saying thickly from lack of use. Petunia waited for another answer from Cirrus but received none. Petunia spoke again after a long silence.

"Why don't I try to teach you how to deal with the Earth obstacle, hm? Will that be okay?"

Stratus still didn't respond, and Petunia desperately wanted to let her do something, but she couldn't force her because in the Earth Kingdom, that would be going against the opportunity of free will. She wanted Cirrus to be willing to do something, and there was the problem.

Since Petunia couldn't force her and Stratus would never make the decision, the two princesses stood there for many minutes being inactive.

Eventually, Petunia knew they needed to do something. She smiled and said, "C'mon, let's go to the Earth obstacle, and I can help you improve."

Cirrus looked at Petunia and nodded once. Petunia was ecstatic at this improvement. She headed toward the obstacle course and made a "follow me" gesture.

She's being really kind to me, Stratus thought. *Why is she doing so to such a low-life person who should have been the one to die and not her twin? Why would this person show such kindness to me? I think she wants me to follow her... No, I shouldn't go. I'm not worthy enough to be with someone that nice. I deserve to remain here alone.*

Petunia was worried, and it was very obvious.

"Cirrus?" she asked. "Are you coming with me? Would you rather teach me instead of me teaching you?"

I can't teach, thought Stratus once more. *Besides, someone as good as she is can't be taught anything else. I'm not worthy to be taught by her either. She has too much to teach me, and we don't have enough time to go over even one-hundredth of it all. I can't accept her kindness; I'm not good enough to. Why can't I have this much good in me? Why can't I be like her? Why—*

Petunia interrupted her thoughts with a hug. Cirrus was caught way off guard. This nice thing was getting to be too much. Why couldn't Petunia allow her to wallow in her thoughts? Why did she have to be so nice? It was starting to ruin autumn. Immediately, Stratus wished she could take those thoughts back. Petunia was being kind. Cirrus should be kind, but that was hard for Stratus.

Cirrus, wanting to correct her thoughts, began walking toward the obstacle course like she knew Petunia wanted. Yes, if she could make Princess Petunia happy, then all would be right once more.

Petunia could hardly hold in her excitement when she saw Stratus acting of her own accord. This was a huge step for her, of which Petunia was particularly joyous about. It wasn't often nowadays Cirrus did…well, anything, really. She mostly kept to herself and said nothing. Sure, she still hadn't said much, but at least she was doing *something*, which was much better than nothing.

Excited, Petunia began their lesson on overcoming the Earth obstacle course.

"All right!" she said with a clap of her hands. "Do you need help with not using your powers, or maybe with just the obstacles? I'm here to help you with whatever it is you may need! Just say the words, and I'll happily help you!"

At this point, Petunia laughed joyously. Stratus thought Petunia was just being too happy, but Cirrus thought she should give Petunia a chance and try to return the kindness, which had been shown to her previously.

"It doesn't matter what we do," Stratus said.

Petunia's eyes widened. Cirrus had spoken! This must truly be a miracle from the Creator Himself! Petunia quickly prayed before continuing the task at hand.

"Well, then," said Petunia, "we shall simply work on using this obstacle course and not using our powers. I won't be using my powers either, so that we'll be doing it together as equals."

But we're not equal and never will be, Stratus thought.

Petunia went to the starting line and waited as Cirrus slowly followed behind.

"Ready?" Petunia asked but received no answer. "Well, you can go whenever you feel comfortable."

If so, thought Cirrus once again, *then I shall never begin because I should never have such a good life that I become comfortable, but I don't want to let Petunia down for she has been so kind to a person who does not deserve it. I wish I could return her kindness. The obstacle course appears the only way. I suppose I should begin it, shouldn't I? I already have many obstacles on my own; I'm not sure I need more. But I need to repay the kindness. I must begin soon. She probably thinks I'm stalling when I just want to be by myself, and I know she'll let me be alone if only I appear to be attempting this course. I'm really not good enough to even be here right now. Oh, how I wish I was not the one to live. I wish—*

Before she realized what was happening, she was running. The tears were streaming down her cheeks like two rivers. She began doing the obstacle course, not even giving it half of her attention. She just wanted to forget her twin right now, but no, she had to have silly ability to remember everything! Why couldn't she have something useful like wisdom or seeing visions or mind reading? If she had any of those, she would be able to help her fellow princesses, but no. She had to have the least useful thing in this situation possible! She wanted to scream and run away from this horrible nightmare. She couldn't, though, because she only wished it to be a nightmare when it was really reality and—

Stratus fell flat onto the ground. Her breathing was very heavy. She wasn't able to go on. She heard nothing but saw Petunia leaving. Cirrus cracked a smile. Ha, she knew Petunia would eventually leave her all alone just like everyone else. It was then Stratus entered pitch-black darkness.

23

Contact

Petunia ran toward Natascha and the male captor who hadn't been paying terribly too much attention toward Princess Cirrus and Princess Petunia since they were best behaved. The captors had been paying more attention toward Princess Currentide and Princess Pyra who seemed to stir up trouble easily.

"Natascha!" Petunia yelled.

Natascha and her partner in crime looked to Petunia. It was very unlike her to yell, especially to her kidnappers.

"What is it?" snapped Natascha. Princess Pyra and Princess Currentide appeared to be doing something very important, and Natascha didn't like it.

Petunia was out of breath and was forced to pause, but she needed to help Stratus.

"Cirrus… She…she…she…"

"Well, spit it out! I don't have all day!"

Natascha's eyes flitted between Princess Petunia and the Princesses of Fire and Water.

"Cirrus fell and…and she—oh, please come look!"

Petunia ran back toward the obstacle course of Earth, merely hoping Natascha was following behind. Something cramped up in Petunia's leg. With a cry of pain, she bent down to hold it. Natascha ran on.

"David, you watch the Earth princess! I'll take care of Princess Stratus!"

"Roger!" David, the other captor, replied. He stooped down to inspect Princess Petunia more closely, for he had recently studied some medicine. As he examined it, his brow furrowed more and more, his worry lines growing increasingly more prominent. He looked quite grave. "This is worse than I thought. Princess Petunia, you won't be able to walk for quite some time."

"What? But no!" she retaliated. "I have to go help Cirrus. She can't just lie there all by herself!"

Petunia desperately tried to stand up, but her efforts proved to be futile. The pain was too great, and David was gently pushing her back to the ground.

I must overcome this pain, she thought to the Creator, *if I ever want to help Cirrus!*

She pushed David away as she attempted to stand up once more. The intensity of the pain was increasing with every movement Petunia made. She used David to balance herself. Once she was standing, she immediately collapsed. David caught her.

Over in the fish tank, Currentide had noticed the lapse of thoughts in both Stratus and Petunia. She looked over at where Natascha was carrying Cirrus toward the male captor and where he, in turn, held Petunia. They both carried the princesses toward the door where they laid them down. Natascha began running toward the tank.

Are you even listening to me? Pyra thought. Currentide shifted her focus. Pyra gave her an annoyed look. *You just missed the greatest plan I think I've ever had because you were too busy—*

Shut up, Currentide commanded, and Pyra obeyed out of a slight fear she was unwilling to show on her face. Currentide spoke to Pyra seriously. *Natascha will be in here any minute, undoubtedly to take us back to our place of captivity. The other two have passed out, but I'm not sure why. I'm starting to worry about them.*

Oh no, Pyra thought. *Don't you go all sappy and sorrowful on me!*

Well, I'm sorry you girls are the closest thing I've ever had to friends in my life!

With that note, she swam to the top of the water where she passed Natascha. Pyra watched from under the water as Natascha swam closer and closer. As Natascha grabbed Pyra and pulled her to the top, Pyra wondered how one could be a princess and not have any friends. She herself had many friends. All one had to do was walk up to anyone of her choosing and introduce herself as the princess of the kingdom, the rightful heir to the throne, and she would have made a friend who would serve her until the very end. So how could this girl from the Water Kingdom not have friends?

Before entering the vehicle, all princesses were blindfolded and their limbs tied together. Pyra and Currentide were given a liquid that knocked them out. When those two awoke the next day, they were in their room with the other two princesses who were sleeping in their beds.

Pyra picked up the lone piece of tungsten from her bed and diminished the fire from it. She proceeded to throw it at Currentide who responded by giving a sleepy look.

"Hey, you," said Pyra. She propped herself upon her hand. "What was that all about with the whole 'no friends' thing yesterday? It's practically impossible to not have friends when you're a princess."

You could never understand, thought Currentide coldly to Pyra.

"Wow, no need to be so dark. Brighten up, will ya?"

Are you saying I need to glow?

Pyra laughed. "Oh, Currentide, you've always had a great sense of humor."

Currentide paused, unsure if she felt confident in what her heart told her to do next.

Do you really *want to know why I don't have friends since it's obviously so easy for you to do so?*

Pyra nodded, confused. "Of course, that's why I asked. Why? Do you think I'm a liar?"

I'm not surprised in the slightest that you tell lies. Your mind supports my theory.

Pyra grumbled, knowing Currentide was telling the truth. The Water princess smiled and looked at the ground. She began the story of her life.

When I was young, before I was yet ten, I would have lessons from teachers my parents provided for me. I'm sure they were great teachers, but I was stubborn. I refused to let them teach me. This resulted in my parents requiring my presence.

The first time it happened, I was ecstatic. I barely got to see my parents and to be able to have them wish to see me and want to talk with me was a blessing in my eyes. So I started to do different things that always got me in trouble with them.

Of course, they knew my intentions since I couldn't keep my mind block up very long at that time. They quickly stopped sending for me. I was devastated and caused my first teacher to quit.

They were furious with me. I was scared out of my wits and have feared them ever since then. That day, I begged them to let me learn with the wealthy families and kids of lords and ladies. I claimed that if I learned with other students, I wouldn't act up.

They agreed, and I was happy for a time. I would finally have friends. As any girl going into double digits, I thought I was the coolest person around. On my first day, the other students all wanted to be my friend just because I was the princess. I was happy because for the first time in my life, I had people who cared for me and I for them. I didn't care if their sole reason was because their parents wanted them to be friends with me simply because in the future, if they were in my good graces, I would most likely make their lives much easier on them and their parents. I knew their parents had the ulterior motives, and they were simply obeying the commands; their minds easily told me that much along with a lot more.

At this point in Currentide's tale, Stratus awoke and curled toward the corner. Pyra continued to stare at Currentide. She continued.

The second year I had gone to that school, if that's what one called it, the girls who I was friends with the previous year ignored me and acted as if I'd been there forever. Instead of hanging out with me, they hung out with a new girl, Sophie. Saying that I was upset is an understatement. These were my friends, and I wasn't about to let them get away with abandoning me.

Did I want them back? To answer your question, not in the slightest. I was not *going to be friends with people who were that disloyal and fickle. And so, I decided to have my revenge.*

At the beginning of the week, I waited patiently for everyone to arrive in the classroom. Once everyone was there, I swam to the front of the room.

"Listen up!" I told them. "I have some announcements to make!"

I proceeded to tell of their deepest and darkest secrets or at least the things they didn't want everyone else to know. In some cases, I told both. I laughed at them as did the rest of the class, unless it was his or her turn to be shamed. That person did not laugh.

After I had embarrassed all in the room save myself, I returned to my regular spot. The teacher came into the classroom and began the lesson for the day. The students gave me occasional glares. Personally, I was satisfied with myself. I hoped this lesson I gave showed them what it's like to feel hurt and rejected.

Once break began, the students called me a jerk and other similar names you wouldn't understand due to the fact you aren't from the Water Kingdom. You wouldn't understand how much it hurts to be called those names. Thankfully, they couldn't reveal any of my secrets, for my mind block was much more advanced than theirs were.

After the initial name-calling, the students simply decided to ignore and shun me. I quickly realized how much worse it was to be alone and with people than alone with none. I sat by myself and strengthened my mind. I spend more and more time in the library now, reading.

Eventually, I couldn't take the pain anymore and approached my parents. I asked them if they would take me out of the classroom and place me in private lessons once more. I told them I didn't like it there anymore.

I knew they were reading my mind during this time, and so they knew exactly what had happened. They told me they felt I had received the punishment I deserved, and that they would place me once more in private lessons.

Currentide paused for a few moments to collect her thoughts before continuing on.

To this day, all I have is my personal assistant who isn't as much of a friend as a servant. Especially since my incident, I've worked extremely hard to hone my ability and power. Although I haven't spent much time on long distance, the length I can hold up my mind block has surpassed many. Only my parents and a select few others are superior.

Of course, I still annoy my teachers and my assistant. How else am I supposed to get my parents to notice anything I do and actually have a conversation with me?

After this, Currentide was silent. Pyra still stared, caught in the trance of Currentide's story. She could easily think of Currentide as an antisocial, considering she didn't speak for the greater part of their stay of being kidnapped. It was understandable that Currentide didn't have friends, but what Pyra couldn't understand was if Currentide wanted friends, then why didn't she try harder? Or why didn't she control their minds to make them want to be her friends? It was obvious to Pyra what Currentide should have done and what she hadn't.

The three sat in silence for some time for Petunia was still asleep.

Currentide…

Currentide shook her head. She was beginning to imagine things that weren't real.

Currentide?

It was growing stronger. She refused to believe her parents were talking to her. It was impossible.

Currentide!

It was a shout now. Currentide jerked her head up. Pyra cocked hers.

"Currentide, wha—" Pyra began but was forced to stop via the mind.

Mom? Currentide thought quietly, hardly daring to believe they'd contacted her. *Dad? Is it really you?*

Currentide! Queen Mizu was joyful now. *Yes, it's us! Oh, we've been searching for you for so long! Where are you?*

King Mul ventured, *Currentide, we know you can't send messages over this long a distance. You're going to have to allow your mind block to shut down. You must become vulnerable and allow us to freely read your mind.*

Tears had begun to flow on Currentide's face. Her parents had been searching for her? They actually *wanted* her back? She began to bawl loud wails. They were so loud they awoke Petunia who had been sleeping the longest. Her leg was wrapped up in something funny and odd.

"Oh, Currentide!"

Petunia kept her left leg, the one she was forced to keep straight now, on her bed as she leaned toward Currentide to hug her in this time which could be grieving or joy. Either way, Petunia knew Currentide needed to know someone was there to love on her.

Petunia sat in silence whilst hugging Currentide, not knowing what to say. It was very loud and caused Cirrus to turn toward the sound.

Once Currentide had calmed down, Petunia asked her a question.

"Do you want to tell me what made you cry?"

Currentide sniffed.

"My-my parents have contacted me, an-and they want me back!"

Petunia cocked her head in confusion, for she had not the slightest idea of which Currentide was speaking of. Pyra, however, knew exactly what it meant.

24

The Story of Cirrus

"You've had outside contact?" Pyra questioned. Her rage started to boil, and she clenched her fists. Fire was forming upon her entire exterior. "How long have you kept this from us? How long have you been doing this, huh? Have you been speaking with these people since we've arrived?"

"No, I just—"

"Don't you speak to me like that! We could've escaped at the very beginning if you'd told us! That or we could have been rescued by them! Ugh! Why did you have to go and be all antisocial?"

"I-I…"

Her father began speaking to her once more. *Currentide, what's going on? Think of where you're located at! How else do you expect us to bring you back home?*

Currentide clapped her hands over her ears in a futile attempt to block out her internal voices. She learned long ago it didn't work, but one could still hope.

We have to know! said her mother. *Where are you located?*

I don't know! Currentide yelled, the tears streaming freely. Oh, this was going to be too much. They wanted her to let her guard down and become vulnerable? She couldn't do it. She wasn't strong enough.

"Currentide," said Petunia. "You are strong enough to overcome whatever is going on with you and your parents. The Almighty Creator is always by your side, willing to do anything with you.

Currentide took in some shaky breaths. *My friends and I escaped once, but we barely saw the outside before we were recaptured. All right?*

There was a pause inside Currentide's head while Pyra was still yelling at her, and Petunia attempted to make Pyra stop.

What do you mean by "we"? her mother questioned.

There are three other girls kidnapped with me.

Who are they?

Currentide wasn't sure how this was relevant but gave her the information she asked for.

There's Pyra the Fire princess, Petunia the Earth princess, and Stratus or Cirrus the Air princess. Why do you need to know?

There was a hiatus given by her parents. Her father severed it. *Are you meaning to say that you were kidnapped with the princesses from the other three kingdoms? Please be as clear as possible on this topic.*

Currentide felt a great need to question her parents but tried her best to think nothing of the sort.

Yes. All four of us were kidnapped. We don't know our location. We've been here for…one moment.

Currentide, we don't have another moment!

She ignored her father for a few seconds in order to retrieve the information she required.

"Stratus!" Currentide commanded, much to Cirrus's surprise. "How long have we been kidnapped?"

"One month, fifteen days, ten hours, thirty-two minutes, and forty-seven seconds and counting," she replied wistfully then lashed out. "Although, why would you need to know?"

Currentide continued her conversation while Petunia, and Pyra gave Stratus confused expressions. The room was very quiet. Pyra wallowed in her anger and Cirrus in her self-pity. Petunia eventually decided to leave Currentide and go to her own bed and begin staring at the strange language once more.

All was quiet as the four were obsessed over their individual things. Occasionally Pyra would have a fight with the wall. The others had come to know this as a regular practice of hers and didn't think too terribly much of it.

After a few days, Natascha came into the room during one of Pyra's fits.

"Princesses," she said, "Today in the obstacle—"

Pyra advanced toward Natascha.

"If you even *dare* to utter a word about those *stupid* obstacle courses, oh, I can promise it won't be pretty. You know those thoughts you have at night that don't allow you to sleep for hours? Well, if we have to do those courses again, I can and will be that, except one hundred times worse."

Natascha stared back at Pyra as if she was about to give her a piece of her mind. However, Natascha turned on her heel and closed the door.

Never again were they taken to the obstacle courses. Instead, they were left alone, locked in their room for days on end. The princesses save Cirrus lost track of the days.

It was growing increasingly closer to winter and thus the princesses were hearing more and more random outbursts from Stratus about how she shouldn't be alive, her hatred of life, anger at the world, and harsh comments on the other princesses.

Petunia was content to stare at the book she couldn't read, continuing to stare at the familiar pictures and wondering if that's how her captors made food. Currentide continued to speak with her parents although it helped none whatsoever. Pyra continued to be angry with Currentide for people of the Fire Kingdom can hold a grudge for a very, very long time, although not always as long as those from the Air Kingdom.

On one particularly quiet day where not one of the princesses had spoken yet, Pyra had one of her outbursts.

"Ugh!" she yelled. "I'm sick and tired of you guys being so boring! I hate my life right now! Currentide refuses to be helpful."

"Hey!" Currentide interrupted. "I'm doing the best I can! At least *I'm* doing something productive. All you do is sit around punching walls. I'm at least trying to get us out of this forsaken place."

"Yes, and *sharing none of the information you've 'supposedly' gathered*."

"Oh, do you want me to share it?"

"I think we'd all like it, you know, just a tiny bit. I don't even care how disadvantageous you think it is."

"Are you asking for a fight? Come at me, let's do it!"

Pyra threw down the piece of tungsten and stood up. Currentide stood up as well. Before anyone got hurt, Petunia jumped up and stood between the Fire and Water princesses.

"Girls, please," she pleaded whilst looking back and forth at their faces. She feared if she didn't, they would begin brawling. "Surely there's a more civil way to settle this? I can get Natascha, and we can make tea and have a nice little chat. Wouldn't that be good? We can talk it out and—"

Pyra shoved her out of the way, burning Petunia's arm in the process.

"Don't get in the way," Pyra growled. "Else, you wish to be pummeled to the ground so deep you're sent back to the day you were born."

Petunia swallowed but knew peace must be brought to this place of evil violence. Holding her arm, she stepped back between them and stared at Pyra directly into her soul. Pyra yelled as fire formed while Currentide created as much water as possible. Petunia flinched as the two were about to attack each other.

"What are you two planning, huh?" came a voice from the corner. "You don't want to…kill each other, do you? If you are out to kill, then I'm the one to do it to. Come on, attack *me,* a willing victim. Don't you want your anger to be diminished? Go ahead."

Pyra and Currentide lowered their arms and elements. Petunia emerged from her cowered state. It was Stratus who had spoken.

"What is this? Why aren't you giving me the pain I deserve? Go on! Kill me already! I was supposed to die anyway, not her!"

Petunia advanced a step toward Stratus with out-stretched arms.

"Cirrus, what's wrong?"

"Step back!" Stratus said in a strong and harsh voice.

Petunia flinched once more. Pyra wasn't going to deal with all this mysterious stuff. Without the mind-reading ability, she was required to get information by force whether it be by physical means, blackmail, or threats.

"Quit dodging around this topic!" Pyra said, equally commanding. "Tell us what the whole 'I'm not supposed to be alive' gimmick is all for. I'm tired of hearing you give us a sliver of information and not the whole story."

Cirrus stared with cold eyes.

She said very quietly so as it was almost inaudible, "I will tell you why I should be dead if you will all be so content as to sit quietly on your respective beds and not interrupt me. If either of these needs isn't met, I will stop speaking and proclaim my story complete."

She waited for any objection while the princesses slowly obeyed. After a few minutes, Stratus began her tale without a single interruption. Although, Pyra had to bite her tongue a few times in order to keep the requirements.

"As you all know, those from the Air Kingdom remember everything. Not a single memory escapes us. We remember everything as if it just happened. There is no way to forget, although, trust me, I've tried.

"When I was younger, I had the best and closest friend a girl could ever wish for. She was my twin, and her name was Cirrus. We were inseparable. Our maid and butler tried 127 times to pull us apart to no avail. We went to the greatest lengths as to stay together.

"Also, we were identical. Not many could tell the subtle difference, save us. I know we were not technically identical since the Creator creates each of His children a different way, but most didn't know the difference.

"Cirrus was easily smarter than me. I knew from an early age she would grow up to be queen, since only one heir can rule. I figured I would stand by her side and simply not rule with her. I was fine with that as I was never good with strategies or mathematics or any of the school work. She was even better at using her powers than me! I knew she had easily surpassed me on the day we were born, and I would never catch up.

"But I wasn't jealous. She was my best friend. One of our wise teachers once told us, 'To be jealous of a friend or any other person is equal to setting up your own funeral.' I took it to heart and vowed not to be jealous of any other single person. I was really good at it too.

"On our tenth birthday, they said it was time. Of course, you have no idea what I'm talking about since you haven't gone through it yourselves.

"Allow me to explain. In each kingdom, there is a committee. This committee rarely has to do anything seeing as how their job is to make sure the queen and king don't break the royal laws. Infractions are rare. Once one happens, the committee steps in and publicizes it. That's part of their job. This is to assure rulers don't break the royal laws, and it works. No ruler would want his or her blunders to be announced and made sure all in the kingdom knew of it.

"Well, I don't know if you've read up on the royal laws or not, but one of them is the king and queen are only allowed one child so as they won't have to worry about the princesses and princes fighting over who was to be the heir.

"This was a problem when Cirrus and I were born. If I'm not mistaken, in this situation the committee was supposed to kill one of us on the spot. However, my parents pleaded they allow us both to live. They reasoned the committee could kill the one who wasn't as intelligent and allow the other one who was more fit for the throne to live. After a debate, the committee agreed with my parents on the condition they kill the dumber one in ten years.

"Our parents didn't give us names. When we were really young, they told us to play a game. They gave us a couple of names and said we could pick which one we liked. We could even switch our names around whenever we wanted to. It was fun for a few years. Then we got a little older and the game became less fun.

"'Mommy! Daddy!' we cried. 'Can we have more permanent names now?'

"'My child,' my mother said, 'please continue to play this game. All will be explained in due time. I promise.'

"So we continued to play this silly game, confusing the castle hands as to which twin we were that day. Cirrus and

I often looked longingly out the windows since our parents wouldn't even let us socialize outside the castle walls.

"We tired of the game once more, so we went to our parents again.

"'Mother! Father!' we cried. 'How much longer will this silly game last?'

"'My child,' my father said, 'please continue to play this game. All will be explained in due time. I promise.'

"We were told about the committee very briefly a couple weeks before our tenth birthday arrived. They said, and I'm paraphrasing, there would simply be some tests on our birthday to see who would rule and become queen later. We were perfectly fine with that, for they didn't tell us about the dying part. When our birthday did come, we were asked to be separated to take the tests. We refused. We screamed at them. We fought them off, and they fought back. They realized they could accidentally kill one of us, and forbid it be the wrong one! They stopped and allowed us to take the tests together.

"Quickly they reset the separate rooms and moved the objects and such into a larger room. Cirrus and I were more excited than ever that we got our way. We had pinky promised years ago never to leave each other's side, no matter what.

"We were taken into the larger room and sat down side by side in front of a table. We performed the tests of which I'm not going to go into detail. Basically, they tested our different skills. The checked our power, ability, capability to create strategies, knowledge of laws, knowledge of kingdoms, mathematics, how we would react to certain situations, and much more.

"Now, I don't have the knowledge of what our scorings were nor how the tests work. All I know is that I must have been worse, which was easily to be expected, for what happened next was something neither of us could have ever prepared for.

"The committee likes spears, and we'd seen the weapons around the castle before, so it didn't surprise us in the slightest that the committee members testing us held spears."

Stratus began shaking very prudently. Tears welled up, prepared to fall, and dripped while she was talking.

"Th-the table had been moved to the side so Cirrus and I ended up standing side by side again. It was then a committee member lunged for me with his spear. It happened quickly, but I managed to cringe away.

"I would have been dead, but no. C-Cirrus was too good for that. She cared a lot for me.

"When the spear was headed for me, she dove. No one had suspected it, not even I: her lifelong friend who'd known her since birth.

"The committee was shocked at the outcome; however, there was no way it could be rewound or fixed. I sat there, holding her body and remembering our promise not to ever leave each other's side. So I kept my promise and stayed with her. Many tried to force us apart, but I refused! They would never make me break our promise."

Stratus sat for a few minutes, collecting herself. Once she felt calm enough to proceed, she did.

"When her funeral came, I asked if we could lay her in the clouds in my room. They abided, considering how I'd been.

"There was one problem, though. Not even the committee was sure which one they had killed. They were merely supposed to kill the one less suited for queendom. They weren't required to know which one of us was which. They'd heard Cirrus was better, but that could easily become irrelevant once the tests began.

"When we had the funeral, I refused to divulge the information about which twin had died.

"Once my studies became harder, I put myself into them more, for Cirrus. I thought maybe by trying to be like her I would ultimately become her. After her death, I devoted most of my time to reading about the committee. I wanted revenge on these evil people. I also ordered to be called by both names so she could be remembered. I never wanted her name to be forgotten. I worried if her name was never mentioned, I wouldn't have kept my promise of us always staying together."

Stratus stared the other princesses straight in the eye.

"This is why I was supposed to die; Cirrus was supposed to live. I live, knowing I can and will never be her. I've wondered over six billion times if I would have dove in front of her if she was being attacked by the committee, but I'll never know now, will I?"

Stratus rolled over on her bed and gave one final warning to the princesses. Could she call them friends?

"Now beware, for winter is coming. I can assure you, I will be an even worse pain than Pyra. There will be no encouragement, only pain."

"Hey!" shouted Pyra. "I take offense to that!"

"It's only the beginning."

"Are you asking me to fight you?"

"Good night, Pyra. It will be the last of many to come."

"What does that mean? Hey, I'm talking to you!"

Pyra shot fire in the same instant of when Stratus put up a shield of air. Pyra groaned and punched the wall some more. There were many holes in it now. Their captors had yet to fix them. Currentide's eyes flicked from princess to princess as she read different minds. Petunia, unsure of what to do next, sat quietly upon her bed and pondered upon Stratus's story as well as the events that had happened thus far today.

This was the only time Stratus had revealed who she truly was, and the first time she'd trusted anyone since Cirrus's death.

25

A Meeting

When contact with Currentide had ceased that night when Currentide fell asleep, King Mul and Queen Mizu frantically began speaking internally to one another.

When shall we tell the others? posed King Mul.

You think they'll believe us? Queen Mizu laughed. *Please! The Fire Kingdom will accuse us of taking their princess. We must get the other two kingdoms on board without forcing their minds. The Fire Kingdom, if not willing to believe the other kingdoms under peer pressure, will then have to be convinced internally.*

Well then, how are we to get the Earth and Air Kingdoms on board with the truth?

Queen Mizu sighed. *Must I come up with all the answers? Well, it'll be easy to get the Earth Kingdom to believe us, but the Air, however… Winter is approaching fast. We need to act now or never. Once winter hits, it will be most hard to communicate and be productive. They won't listen, nor will they allow us to speak freely.*

There was a space of silence as King Mul was thinking. As their minds were one, Queen Mizu knew exactly what he was thinking without even having to read his mind.

No! she protested. *We can't do that! It hasn't been performed for generations, nor will we be the ones to bring it back! It cannot and will not be done; I refuse for you to even suggest it to the other queens and kings. No, don't you say that next!*

King Mul disobeyed his wife and spoke his idea. It appeared to be the most obvious choice to him.

If we go through with it, just think of how much simpler communication would be. We wouldn't have to send mind messages nor have to deal with the other Kingdoms' messengers. We could all speak together in one place! The worst the other kingdoms can do is say no.

Yes, argued Queen Mizu, *or we can be the beginning of another war, and I refuse to have the Water Kingdom be the ones to bring it up. What happens if it comes back? What happens if another war arises? We don't have trained soldiers for this. Think of what it would cost our people, Mul. Think about those we rule over. What would it cost them?*

And what has it already cost us? Mul challenged. *What of our daughter? It's not as if the committee will allow us to have another child. They'll wonder what will happen if Princess Currentide returns. Then what? We can't afford to lose our daughter, Mizu. We can't afford losing the heir or our sanity.*

We don't have much more time left to rule. Soon it will be Currentide's turn to rule the Water Kingdom. She'll be able to change whatever she wants, so why shouldn't we take the risk of starting a war? Our daughter is at stake here.

And, he continued, *there is the chance she won't want to have a war with the princesses she's been kidnapped with.*

Queen Mizu pointed a problem out, *Unless the other princesses care more about hurt to their family's pride over a bond formed and fallen.*

King Mul did not have a response to this for some minutes. He knew what must be done, but his wife disagreed with him. The people of the Water, Earth, Fire, and Air Kingdoms had never heard of the word "divorce" before. It had never happened nor was it ever even thought of. The couple was forced to live together, so they might as well try to make it work. In the case of the king and queen, the marriages were arranged, and unhappy rulers led to an unhappy kingdom.

Finally, King Mul replied. *You know we have to take the risk. There is no other way—*

Tears began rolling down Queen Mizu's cheeks. *We can find another way, Mul! We can figure something out, can't we? Surely it isn't too terribly hard. I'm sure we can try…*

Queen Mizu stopped speaking and left the room, knowing full well that didn't stop the conversation. She swam toward a balcony and stood there staring at the night fish. They were very beautiful creatures; Mizu might even call them more unfathomable than the day fish. In the middle of her moment of solemnity and peace, she was given a message by her husband.

Swiftly now! We must catch them off guard when they're too tired to question us!

The Water queen simply shook her head and laughed. He didn't fail to randomly remind her why she loved him. She swam to meet him outside the castle. Most of their citizens were asleep at this hour, so they didn't fear bothering anyone.

Where shall we tell them to meet? the queen asked, then seeing her husband's thoughts, proceeded. *Oh! I see. Yes, we shall call them all there. I'd almost forgotten about that. Perfect!*

They swam along their merry way, all the while calling their fellow rulers to meet in secret.

Finally coming to their senses, the rulers of the Fire Kingdom began to retaliate. In addition to becoming themselves again, they realized their location. All eight rulers stood around a table the Earth Kingdom started making. The kings and queens were on a small island in between the Fire and Earth Kingdoms. This was where the rulers met before the War.

"Why are we here?" King Hwajae commanded. "In my land of all places!"

"Technically," Queen Mizu challenged, "we're not in anyone's land. It's simply *near* your land."

"Yes, but I was told about it nearly months ago! I sent an exploration team out to claim it and—"

"Dearest Hwajae," Queen Kasai growled through clenched teeth, "I thought we agreed not to tell the other rulers."

"Too late now."

Queen Kasai heavily sighed, not entirely content or happy with her husband at the moment.

Queen Kūki, who was massaging her temples, softly demanded, "Please do tell us why the Water Kingdom has called us here on this frightful night. Gong-Gi and I were sleeping peacefully until you bothered us with your awkward mind messages. I would very much like to go back to sleep, but I know the rest of you will prevent me from doing so."

"And I know I'm not mistaken, but isn't what we're doing now what started the War?" King Gong-Gi of the Air Kingdom piped up.

Queen Mizu sighed internally; her daughter had to get it from somewhere. For her sake, King Mul explained.

"Yes, we realize this is what most scholars say started the war," he answered. "However, for a couple of reasons, we find this necessary. One of our reasons is Queen Mizu and I recently had contact with our daughter and—"

"Oh, sure," said King Hwajae annoyingly, "just use your magical mind-reading ability to talk with your daughter. Don't even ask if we'd like to know what happened to our daughters. Simply let us go find them ourselves. I bet—"

"Do you realize we know where your daughters are at as well?" Queen Mizu hissed.

Silence commenced. The hush was obvious as the rulers sorted this piece of information out. Unexpectedly, the Earth Kingdom spoke first, knowing from their own experience the Fire Kingdom would accuse those of the Water Kingdom.

"Are they together?" Queen Chikyū asked, worry lines showing prominently upon her face. Mul nodded; Chikyū sighed happily. "So they were kidnapped together and are being held captive together."

"Correct," Mul answered.

"That is," said Queen Kūki. "Assuming they're all still alive."

"That last time we made contact was right before this meeting."

"Yes, and how much time does one need in order to kill another person?" She snapped her fingers. "Just that long is all it takes."

"Like you would know," Kasai replied with a roll of the eyes.

"Have you forgotten one of my daughters was taken away from me six years ago?" Kūki was very angry now and banged her fist upon the table as she spoke those words.

Another silence followed. This was an easy task to do considering the four kingdoms rarely talked to each other.

King Jigu spoke. "So where are they?"

Mizu and Mul stared at the table, avoiding the oncoming gazes from the other rulers.

"We're not sure," Mul admitted. "That's the problem. Our daughter, Currentide, isn't quite sure where they're at. She's relayed many events that have happened there, and it's all very confusing.

"However, we *have* gathered that they aren't in any of the four kingdoms. On a whim, we tried searching for her mind outside of the kingdoms when we found her. She's relayed almost everything possible, trying to exclude no details, but it hasn't done any good. The things she's described… I've never heard of them before.

"For example, Princess Stratus or Cirrus of the Air Kingdom has proclaimed how the air is more difficult to breathe. Princess Petunia of the Earth Kingdom has cried over lifeless plants. Princess Pyra of the Fire Kingdom has destroyed a bed to fend of the cold. Our own Princess Currentide cannot read the minds of her captors. Forgive me if I'm wrong, but have any of you ever heard of such a place?"

The other rulers shifted uncomfortably. None had heard of such a foul and vulgar place. The things King Mul described were simply unthinkable and unheard of in their kingdoms. They all wondered who would want to live in that forsaken place; it sounded horrid.

"How are we to save them if we don't know their location?" Queen Chikyū asked.

"We don't," King Gong-Gi said bluntly. "There are too many things we don't know, and we simply don't have the time to go looking ourselves. We have the kingdoms to think about."

"And," added King Jigu, "I don't like the idea of sending our people to explore a territory we have no knowledge of. They could all be killed or worse."

"We can't just stand by and do nothing!" Queen Kasai shouted.

"What else *is* there to do?" Kūki retorted. "There is nothing, I tell you nothing, that the kingdoms haven't already tried."

"Hmph. If that's the truth, then we'll simply have to wait for our daughters to return to us. I certainly hope that's all right with the rest of the kingdoms considering the fact that coronation days are coming soon. Our daughters are supposed to be prepared to coronate and rule an entire kingdom. Surely it will work out just perfectly without heirs! Oh, there'll be games and—"

"Silence!" commanded King Gong-Gi. "We want our daughter back just as badly as you do."

"Oh, yeah?" King Hwajae challenged, wanting to be part of the argument. "Well, is *your* daughter the *heir to the throne*?"

The rest of the rulers resided to stare at him. Mizu rubbed her forehead and temples. She commented to Mul, *I'm going to venture out and say that* this *is the reason why the meetings stopped, and the War started.*

Mul smiled and laughed internally at her.

"What?" Hwajae questioned. "Usually someone would have spoken by now, but I guess you all are too star struck by a king's presence that you aren't entirely sure how to act.

"The appropriate way would be to bow very low to the ground. Now, I can't demonstrate for you since I'm royalty, but if anyone would like to volunteer I'd be glad to critique them—"

King Hwajae turned toward his wife who was glaring daggers straight into the very core of his soul. He didn't show how much pain she had caused him for that was part of the Fire Kingdom's way.

"So what *are* we going to do, seeing as how we've yet to reach a conclusion?" King Jigu pointed out. "We know they aren't *in* any of the kingdoms, which makes me wonder where exactly they are being kept, who would do this and why? If they know how much trouble they'll get in, why would they commit such a crime in the first place?"

"Maybe 'they' aren't from any of the kingdoms," said King Mul.

"That's preposterous!" Queen Kasai exclaimed. "There was no mention whatsoever in the Creation story about any other kingdoms. Are you accusing the Creator of being a liar? Think of our ancestors who have carefully passed down this story! And why are we saying the kidnapper is multiple people? We don't know that. There could have very well have been a single person to pull this off."

"Your second question is so ridiculous I'm not even going to answer it," said Queen Kūki.

"And," added Queen Chikyū, "we can't say there weren't other kingdoms in the beginning. Maybe they weren't mentioned in the Creation story because they were purposely left out. It could have been order to protect us and the generations to come. Maybe they're harmful and commit acts such as kidnappings."

She had a point, and the others saw it.

"Well," argued Queen Kasai since she couldn't resist being wrong, "you can't prove that."

"Technically," Queen Mizu said, "we can. We've already been sending out search parties, haven't we? So why not just send them outside the kingdoms? King Jigu, I know you don't like that idea, but if we were all willing, we could send our search parties together."

"No," King Gong-Gi retaliated. "It cannot be known to others that we met up here tonight. Our people must be kept in the dark lest we want them to think another war is brewing about. Also, we'll be able to cover more ground if our kingdoms search separately."

"We can also keep tabs on each other via Mizu and Mul," said King Jigu. "They can relay to the rest of us how the searches are going. I'm sure you two have been reading our minds already, so if you can, please send us messages honestly. We want our daughters back too."

"You what?" King Hwajae shouted, furious. "How long have you been reading our minds?

"Yes, we'll certainly make sure to do that, King Jigu," King Mul replied, completely ignoring Hwajae's question.

"Then it's settled!" Queen Chikyū exclaimed. "We'll all send out search parties outside of the kingdoms and hope for the best. Maybe one of them will stumble upon the place of keeping where our daughters lie."

"Or better yet," said Queen Kasai, "they'll escape on their own."

On that note, the kings and queens all left the starry darkness and headed toward their respective kingdoms.

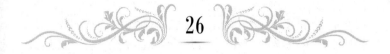

26

Short Tempers

Stratus, who was propped upon her elbow, sighed.

"Currentide, can't you do something useful for once and actually *tell* us what's going on at home? I mean, seriously, what's the good of mind reading if you can't get anything good out of it when you need to?"

They'd been locked up for another week, easily enjoying one another's company.

"Do you realize that I can control your mind whenever I want to?" she retorted. "So for you, I could make you imagine Cirrus was still here, and you would wholeheartedly believe it. Your reaction to it once she 'disappeared' would be a moment I might hold very dear to my heart."

"Currentide!" Petunia exclaimed. "That was very mean. I know I'm not to say what you should and shouldn't do, but—"

"Oh, yeah?" Pyra interjected, wanting to one-up them. "Well, *I* can see what happens in the future."

Stratus rolled her eyes. "Dearest Pyra, we all know that you can't choose the moments, though. I mean, when we escaped a month ago, that was the most untimely moment to receive one. If that hadn't happened, we probably could have escaped and wouldn't have had to stay in the wretched place as long as we currently have."

She sighed dramatically, while Currentide realized what those words meant.

Oh! she thought. *Why didn't I think of it before? That was* obviously *a vision! Curse myself for not remembering that book! It's a good thing Stratus can't read minds or else she'd know that I didn't know.*

"So what was your vision of?" Currentide questioned Pyra, now having gotten used to speaking aloud more often.

Pyra stared at the ground. She always felt awkward when speaking about visions, but adding the fact of telling and explaining it to people who had never had a vision before made it that much more of an awkward situation.

"Well, you see, visions… They're kind of like… It's like this… Oh, who am I kidding trying to explain them to you guys!

"A vision can be crystal clear, but when I was younger, they were often blurry. Sometimes they're both. Also, you can be in the vision and seeing the vision at the same time. It's like, as of right now, I'm sitting on my bed, but when I received the vision, I could be overhead or standing somewhere else in the room. Is this making any sense at all?"

Petunia slowly spoke, choosing her words carefully. "So you're saying when you receive a vision, the image you're looking at could contain you, and it's all okay?"

"Precisely!" Pyra exclaimed, excited that another princess understood. Petunia's understanding allowed Pyra to speak more easily. "When you receive a vision, you can also think your own thoughts. However, you're not allowed to choose the length of the vision. You also can't touch anything. It's like you're a ghost, and your hand floats through objects and people."

"Oh, brother," Stratus sighed. "You seriously believe in all that mumbo jumbo about ghosts? Let me guess, you also believe in 'supernatural beings' and monsters coming to get you in your sleep."

Pyra gave her an annoyed look.

"I think I liked you a lot better in the fall," she commented.

"Oh, no, just wait until spring. It'll be like two Petunias but worse."

Petunia's mouth opened but quickly closed as she stared into her hands.

"Continuing on," said Pyra, "in the vision I received when we almost escaped, I saw the four of us in a different room. The room was slightly blurry but had more colors. I think the base colors were red, white, green, blue, and… brownish gray? Anyway, I saw the four of us, and another girl. She felt very different, and I wasn't entirely sure why... I'm remembering there *was* something prominently different about her, but I don't know what it was. Ugh! It's making me want to—"

She was cut short as she proceeded to punch the wall. The others sat as Stratus commented.

"Yes, Pyra punches walls because that always solves her problems."

"Would you rather I punch you?" Pyra screeched.

"Ha!"

Stratus began to laugh. Pyra was frozen in midair and looked as if she was fighting against strings that were pulling her back.

"Yes, because our little friends will allow you to hurt me. Oh, I wish you could stay like that forever. It's a really good look for you."

Stratus began laughing again.

"C'mon, Currentide! Let me at her! You know you want to see her face pummeled to the ground. At least let me bruise her!"

Currentide shook her head. Petunia stood up angrily.

"Oh! If you two continue fighting, how are we ever expected to escape from here? So you might as well suck it up and *try* to like each other until we get out of here. Then you can go back to fighting and all can be right in the world!"

The others simply stared at her, mouths agape. Never once had Petunia had such an outburst. The room was silent as Petunia gathered herself once more, sat on her bed, and held her head in her knees. She apologized to both the Creator and the other princesses and promised she would try her best so it would never happen again. Stratus laughed at this.

"Hahaha! Why are you apologizing? It was refreshing to see you get worked up. Although, based upon your previous actions, I doubt you'll do something like that again."

"Do you ever shut up in the winter?" Pyra questioned. "Because if you don't, I'm going to seriously—"

"Seriously what?" Stratus asked with a twinkle in her eye.

"I would have told you, except you interrupted me!" she snapped.

Stratus rolled onto her back and placed her hands behind her head. She sighed.

"I'm going to get bored really fast if we don't get out soon."

"Oh no. Please, let us think of a plan before Stratus decides to go all crazy on us. It would be terrible if my life ended because of some girl from the Air Kingdom."

"What's that supposed to mean?"

"I think I'll just let you wonder for a while."

At this point, Petunia had practically lost hope in trying to make peace between Pyra and Stratus. So she brought out the book she still couldn't read and once again stared at its contents. She felt she could understand the pictures if only she could read the language. It was quite the hindrance for her. She'd already asked, and none of the others could read it. What she did most of the time was stare at the pictures and make up words, all the while pretending she knew exactly what was happening in them.

Eventually, Stratus got bored with Pyra and began searching the room for something. Pyra yelled at her, and Stratus ignored her. The dresser proved to have nothing useful, and the beds were obviously of no help. She walked over to the mirror and cocked her head. This would be sufficient. She pulled back and punched it, causing the shards to shatter everywhere.

The noise was enough for the other three princesses to stop in their tracks. Blood resided upon Stratus's hand. She reached down and picked a piece up. It fit nicely in her hand.

"No!" Currentide shouted before anything had really yet to happen.

Stratus smirked. "Oh? You don't like my thoughts? Well, it's quite upsetting me, and I cannot handle it any longer. Besides, in the Air Kingdom, we do it every winter."

"But you simply can't do that! It's too—"

"I can, and I will."

Petunia and Pyra were getting worried. They both thought Stratus was going to hurt or kill Pyra in some way.

They wondered why Currentide was so worked up about it. Why hadn't she used her mind ability to stop her?

Stratus's hand tensed on the broken piece. New blood flowed. Her reflection copied her movements. She looked just like Cirrus. A tear rolled down Stratus's cheek. Pyra tensed as well, ready to defend herself. Petunia's hands were to her mouth, knowing that with what little life there was in the wardrobe, she wouldn't have enough time to make plants and control them. Currentide was a mess all on her own, wailing about how wrong it was for Cirrus to do this.

Stratus began moving. In one swift motion, she used the shard from the mirror and…cut her hair to her chin.

"Ah," she sighed. "Much better. Now it's not all over me anymore."

She dropped the mirror shard; her hand began healing. She walked back over to her bed and lay down. Currentide was practically in tears.

"That's it?" questioned Pyra. "All she was doing was cutting her hair?"

Currentide nodded.

"That's the entire reason for your random outburst? She wasn't going to attack me?"

Currentide shook her head. "B-but it was so beautiful…" she mumbled. "She shouldn't have just cut it all off like that."

"Oh, please," intercepted Stratus. "It'll be back in the spring, you sissy. You'd never survive as someone from the Air Kingdom."

It was at this moment Natascha walked in. Petunia, in surprise, quickly put her book away.

"Hey, I came to...take you to get...fresh...air," she said, gradually slowing down. "Should I ask why the mirror is broken or why the Air princess's hair is all over the floor? And, um, I'm actually going to ask this, um why is there blood all over the mirror shards?"

Stratus sighed.

"Why do you wimps make it such a big deal that I cut my hair? I mean, seriously, all I did was destroy that which annoys me. Is that such a crime?"

Natascha straightened herself. "As your captor, I must know what goes on in this room. Of course, we have ways, but sometimes I just like to see if you'll tell the truth if I ask you."

She turned on her heel and started for the door.

"Um, excuse me, Ms. Natascha, but do we still get a breath of fresher air?" ventured Petunia.

Natascha snapped her hand.

"Oh, I'd nearly forgotten. Thank you for reminding me, Princess Petunia. You may come first."

"Well, I-I'm sure others have to go worse than I."

"Princess Petunia, I order you to come with me."

"Yes, ma'am."

Petunia stood up off her bed and followed Natascha out the door.

"*I* remembered..." Stratus mumbled.

Natascha led Petunia down the stairs and through the hall. She was steered to an open window. It was an odd custom for Natascha to blindfold each princess. None of them understood it and a couple tried to peek around the blindfold. Natascha was quick to reprimand them, however, so their attempts proved to be useless.

When Petunia and Natascha were finished, the blindfold was taken off. Petunia gazed at the library, wishing desperately their exploration days were back. Petunia really wanted to have another book but didn't want their captors to know she had it.

Natascha turned around, realizing Petunia wasn't following her. Natascha smiled, knowing what Princess Petunia was thinking.

"You want another book, don't you?"

Petunia let out a little gasp, and she blushed, surprised. "Y-you know about the book?"

Natascha laughed. "Dear Princess, we know everything. Why wouldn't we know Princess Currentide stole a book for you three months ago, and you kept it and almost religiously stared at its pages?"

Petunia looked away, ashamed she stared at it that often. She must look at it less and think of the Creator more, that was the answer.

Natascha put all her weight on one leg and placed her hands on her hips.

"Well, do you want another book or not?"

"What? I thought you were going to punish me for having the first book. Is this some form of...reverse psychology, I believe it's called?"

"Look, you're either getting the book or not. Which is it?"

Petunia debated. On one hand, if she received another book, she could compare the two side by side. Maybe Stratus would help her by memorizing them. On the other hand, what if she really *would* get into trouble by receiving a book? That couldn't end well for any of the princesses, and it would most likely make matters worse.

"Natascha, I think I will go get another book."

Natascha smiled, but it didn't reach her eyes. "Excellent."

Well, sometimes risks needed to be taken.

27

The Greater Escape

After Natascha unlocked the door leading to the library, Petunia entered. She was once more surrounded by books. Under normal circumstances, Petunia would have loved to be this close to books. There, Petunia could still feel the life of the plants in them, telling her their stories. When the four kingdoms still traded, books had been made in the Earth Kingdom and sent out to the Water Kingdom and Air Kingdom. Nowadays, the Water and Air Kingdom were forced to cope with what old books they had.

In this library, however, Petunia couldn't even feel life in them. It was so far removed she felt almost as if the plants in the books were dead, if there were any left. The books made Petunia want to hold them all close to her and comfort any plants possibly deep inside.

In the Earth Kingdom, whenever Petunia entered a library, the plants were whispering their contents. Now, when she entered the library, there was silence. No plants called out to her. The only sounds were those of Natascha's breathing and her own.

Petunia browsed through the selection of books available. She would stare at the spines, occasionally choosing one that interested her. When one did spike her interest, she would pull it out, look at the cover, flip through the pages, and put it back. She was in there for some time when Natascha interrupted her browsing.

"Princess Petunia, we must be getting back because your fellow princesses are starting to get weird ideas of what you're doing. Is there any kind of specific book you would like?"

Petunia thought for some moments. She could get a book on escape, but that would be too obvious. Maybe she should get a book on the water creatures or how fire in this world worked or on air flow or something. Or maybe a fairytale book to provide them some entertainment. Oh, but none of them would know how the stories went. Perhaps if they made them up as they looked at the pictures? Petunia, knowing she was running out of time, made a decision. It was farfetched, but in an unknown place, many things can happen.

"Do you have a book," she said, "with a list of words? A list that has all words, so to speak. Am I making any sense at all?"

"Are you saying you want a dictionary?" Natascha replied.

"What is this *dictionary* of which you speak?"

Natascha sighed and walked over to a shelf. It was a very thick volume. She brought it over to Princess Petunia and heaved it into Petunia's hands. Petunia opened it and looked at the pages.

"Is this what you were looking for?"

Natascha's hands rested on her hips, not wishing at all to carry the book back to the shelf. She desperately wished it was what Petunia had been looking for.

Petunia, on the other hand, wasn't entirely sure what it was. The pages still made no sense, but Natascha looked tired from carrying it over to Petunia, and the princess didn't want her captor to have to take it back.

"I'm sure it is similar to what I was originally looking for. Thank you very much. May we go back to the room now?"

Natascha followed Princess Petunia back to the room, keeping a close eye in case she tried to escape. The Earth princess had thus far been the best behaved, but one could never be too cautious when it came to having kidnapped four princesses.

They entered the room, and Pyra left to get fresh air next.

"Oh, great," Stratus groaned. "You have *another* book? What, are you going to stare at these pages and continue to pretend you know what it says? C'mon, we all know you can't read whatever this language is."

"This book's very different from the last one," Currentide commented.

"What do you mean by different?"

"It looks to be a list of words or something."

"I think that's what it is," Petunia said. "Natascha called it a dictionary, but I'm unsure of the meaning of that word. I thought if I could read the list of words, then I could read my other book. However, I still don't know how to say the words."

Petunia's eyes were downcast; she was sad and a little upset she couldn't read these books.

"Let me see if I can figure out how to read this... dictionary?" Currentide stumbled on the new word. "I've read a lot of books, so maybe I can figure something out."

Currentide became content with sitting on her bed and staring at the new book.

Natascha and Pyra quickly came back, and Currentide left. As soon as the door was closed, Stratus grabbed the book and looked at the pages. She turned them as fast as she could, wanting to get as much in before Currentide came back.

"Stratus, what in the kingdoms are you doing?" Pyra questioned.

"Petunia, tell her!" Stratus hissed.

Petunia was caught off guard but obeyed nonetheless.

"Well, after I got a breath of fresher air, Natascha allowed me to grab a book from the library. I ended up with a list of words of which Natascha called a dictionary. Currentide was reading it until—"

"Now I'm memorizing as much as possible since I can do it much faster than Currentide ever will," Stratus said quickly. "This way I can prove my point, *and* we can pretend we're accomplishing something. It's most definitely a win-win situation."

Stratus would have rolled her eyes at this time, except she was too busy glancing at the pages of the dictionary. When Currentide walked in, Pyra attempted to cover for Stratus taking the book. Immediately after Stratus left, Pyra began speaking.

"You know, girls, I'm tired of being stuffed in here. I say we try to escape once again!"

"And what?" Currentide challenged with satire. "Get caught again? I'm sure we would just have a *marvelous* time doing that. Oh, yes, why not? Let's all leave this wretched place and come back. It sounds so delightful that I can hardly wait."

Pyra gave her a look.

"I'm just saying if we're more cautious this time, maybe we won't get caught. We need more of the element of surprise. If we catch them off-guard we can—"

At this moment, the door opened, revealing Natascha and Stratus. Currentide knew Pyra's line of thinking and followed suit. As Pyra began physically attacking Natascha with punches and kicks, occasionally with fire atop them,

Currentide took the water out of her jug and surrounded Natascha's face with it, in the hopes it would throw her off, or something.

"Oh, are we fighting our captors?" Stratus asked. "All right!"

Stratus, too, began fighting Natascha. She brought giant gusts of air to knock Natascha down, all the while laughing maniacally. Petunia simply stood in the doorway, both books in hand, and watched. She didn't like fighting.

Natascha tried to fight back. Sometimes a punch or kick would hit Pyra, but it didn't happen often. When it did, one had to have been paying extreme attention for Pyra never reacted.

Quickly, Natascha was lying on the ground.

"Hurry!" Pyra exclaimed. "Someone grab the things from a bed."

Petunia traded the books for Stratus's bed things and hurried over.

"Who can tie really tight knots?" Pyra asked. "Anyone? Hurry, before she wakes back up or something!"

"I can," said Petunia softly.

"Well, get over here! We need to leave swiftly now."

Petunia obeyed.

"You!" Pyra pointed to Stratus. "Can you let us ride on air or something? They've built new windows, but surely fire can break through."

"Tch," said Stratus, arms crossed and looking away. "You doubt my abilities. Of course we can ride the air, what kind of question is that?"

Just as Petunia was finishing the knots, Pyra was burning the cover on a window.

"Well," Pyra said to Stratus in the middle of her struggle. "Considering last time we tried doing that you wouldn't, I figured I might as well check again. Man, what are these covers made of?"

"It was fall, you dummy! Of course, I wouldn't do anything! Have you learned *nothing* since we've been cooped up in that room?"

"I don't know, aren't you the one who remembers everything?"

"Ugh!"

Stratus crossed her arms and turned away. Her hair flipped a little in addition.

Finally, the cover over the window had melted enough for them to exit.

"Guys, c'mon!" said Pyra. "Stratus, you go first and prepare the air."

"Pfft, 'prepare the air,' she says," Stratus muttered while exiting the building all the same. "As if one 'prepares' air. One day I'm going to…"

Pyra ushered the other princesses out, telling them to hurry and move swiftly now. Currentide jumped out first after finding where Stratus was sending the winds by reading her mind. Petunia held her breath as she watched Currentide jump. She didn't know where to land and hoped Currentide did. Petunia began breathing normally once she saw Currentide was okay.

"Jump to where I'm standing!" Currentide called over the wind. Petunia obeyed. To Stratus, Currentide sent, *Is there any way to make these winds quieter?*

"Well, I'm sorry," Stratus retorted. "It's not *my* fault that in order for us all to comfortably stand the winds have to be plentiful, which equals them being loud."

Currentide shook her head and looked toward the only open window where Petunia was looking at also. Pyra crouched in the window very catlike and jumped. She fell short of the air current and began to fall. Petunia gasped, and her hands flew to her mouth. Currentide didn't appear worried at all for she knew what was on Pyra's mind. Stratus nonchalantly inspected her fingernails.

Pyra used fire to boost herself up onto the winds.

"All good?" Petunia asked. "Are we all set and ready to head home now?"

The girls smiled at the thought of home, even Stratus. To be honest, they'd missed it terribly in the months they'd been gone and kidnapped. They were ready to go back.

"Stratus," Pyra said, "take us home."

"Oh, that would be simply marvelous," said Stratus. "If only one of us knew where we were and how to get there.

Are you kidding me? Not a single one of us knows where we are."

"Could we ask someone how to get back?" ventured Petunia.

Stratus laughed.

"Don't make me laugh," she scoffed. "Don't you remember that over a minute ago we escaped from being kidnapped? Oh, yes, we'll just ask the dark line on the ground for directions. Perfect plan!"

"Can't we just head in *some* direction before our kidnappers see us?" Currentide exclaimed. "Seriously, use some logic for once!"

Stratus mumbled as she guided the air to take them away from the place of which they had recently escaped. First, she simply rose higher whilst moving away. Upon seeing a very large and dark gray path, she traveled toward it. She looked at both horizons. She decided going right would be best for no apparent reason. She followed the path for hours, and there wasn't a soul in sight. Eventually, the princesses figured out they could sit on the air, and all would be fine. Stratus, on the other hand, stood behind them to guide the air since she preferred this method.

To pass the time, Petunia, Pyra, and Currentide discussed their next move with the occasional comment from Stratus, which was usually ignored. They eventually decided when they came to the town, before it became late, they would stop and see what they could find out about their location and the like. From there, they would make yet another plan. If they didn't reach the town, however, they would stop on the strange and large dark gray thing underneath them.

As twilight was approaching them, Stratus began yawning.

"I'm beat. Can we stop now?" she asked. "Wait, why am I asking? I'm the one controlling the winds right now!"

She brought them to the ground and immediately laid down and fell asleep. Pyra rolled her eyes.

"I can't believe we have to sleep on this hard thing, but I guess it beats being kidnapped."

She, too, fell asleep quickly. Currentide lay awake for some time but was so quiet Petunia hadn't noticed she was still awake. Petunia proceeded to pray aloud to the Creator, thinking no one else was listening.

"Dearest Creator," she said. "Thank you for providing us with what we had when we were in the clutches of Natascha and David. I pray You keep us safe tonight. I pray Your will be done as we try to find our way back home, and that we ultimately do find our way back with Your help. In Your name I ask these things. Amen."

Currentide figured it was best, based upon the thought process of Petunia, to say nothing about overhearing Petunia for now.

28

Traveling

"I told you to watch more carefully, idiot!"

"You know how I feel about using the bathroom in front of the cameras!"

"Oh yeah, as if the cameras can see you. How many times do I have to remind you *you're watching what's happening, and they can't see you?*"

"Of course, I know that! It just feels wrong since they're all girls…"

Natascha sighed.

"Don't massage me," she commanded. The machine stopped. She said sarcastically, "So, mastermind, what do you suggest we do next?"

"Well," David started, "we could hack into cameras around the kingdom."

"Too obvious."

"We could also go search for them ourselves."

"Too much work."

"I guess we could ask around?"

"No."

"Send an army?"

"How obvious are you trying to be?"

"What if we went in the plane and searched overhead?"

"Now why—" Natascha stopped abruptly. "That's actually not such a bad idea. Shall we leave now?"

"Can it wait until tomorrow? I really want a full night's rest."

"Ugh, what's up with you and sleep?"

David did his best to shrug.

"Fine," said Natascha, giving in easily. "We'll postpone searching for them. Our technology is easily faster than their powers."

David nodded and left the control room. Natascha, on the other hand, stayed and replayed the princesses' grand escape. She wanted the computers to analyze it, so it may never happen again, once they were back in Natascha and David's hands, that is.

The four elemental princesses awoke to loud beeping and whirring noises. Pyra felt a great headache upon her.

"What is that dreadful noise?" she asked.

For some odd reason, she was the first to awake that day. As she slowly sat up, her sight was becoming clearer.

She blinked several times and even rubbed her eyes as she watched the moving objects all around her. They moved fairly fast, but all of them maneuvered around the princesses.

In fright, Pyra had been stuttering. She now vigorously shook the others awake.

"Guys, guys, guys, guys, guys, guys, guys, guys, guys, guys."

"What in the kingdoms are you talking about?" Stratus groaned, still lying down with her eyes closed. "I was sleeping peacefully until you had to wake me up."

"Just shut up and look around you!"

Stratus shook her head and finally opened her eyes. She joined Currentide and Petunia in the pose consisting of a dropped jaw and wide eyes.

"Oh," Stratus replied, sounding small. "Well, I guess that's our cue to leave."

The objects were several shades of gray, with the occasional black one. The longer the princesses watched, the more they saw. They noticed there were people inside of these moving objects; however, all they saw of the people were faces. The objects also did not touch the ground; the princesses were fine with this aspect considering how they had traveled the previous day. The objects looked like people who were sitting, but the princesses knew that to be untrue considering how large the projectiles were.

"So," said Stratus, "I'm thinking we all jump, and I allow the air to carry us away from this strange place."

The others nodded. After a count off, the four girls jumped, and as Stratus said, the air raised them high above the objects. Once the obstruction was moved out of the way, traffic flowed freely beneath them. The girls continued onward in the opposite direction of where the objects were coming from.

"Um," Currentide pointed out. "If these...people things are going *away*, shouldn't we, too, be going in the other direction?"

"Pfft," said Stratus as she blew her off. "The good part has yet to come, my friend. Surely it will get interesting once we arrive at wherever it is they are leaving. Besides, if it looks too dangerous, although danger can be quite fun, we'll see it from a long ways away simply because we have this amazing thing called an 'aerial view.' You poor souls in the Water Kingdom do not have such a thing."

"Actually, if you swim at the top of the water, you can easily—"

"No, no. You of the Water Kingdom do not believe in aerial view. Nothing you say or do will change my mind."

Currentide glared at her, seriously debating on whether or not to attempt to go into Stratus's mind and change it. She wasn't entirely sure what her parents would say if she *did* manage to do it successfully.

Her parents! She hadn't thought them since they escaped.

Um, hi, she thought awkwardly, hoping her parents would hear her. She most definitely did not like her lack of ability to send messages across large distances. She must work on it once she was back home and in a familiar setting. She figured she could practice with Flowon. He wouldn't enjoy it.

Currentide? her parents sent. *Oh, we haven't contacted you in a couple of days, haven't we? Things have been really crazy here in the kingdoms, and we've been really busy.*

Sure, busy, Currentide thought sarcastically and immediately regretted it. *I didn't mean to say that…*

Her parents said nothing in reply. She had forgotten whatever she thought would be "sent" to her parents. Had she not stopped herself, she would have thought, *Sure, busy. You've probably just forgotten to contact your daughter. Don't worry, I completely understand.*

Okay, Currentide thought, *we escaped yesterday—*

Yesterday! they exclaimed. *Why didn't you contact us? We could've narrowed down your location more.*

And you can't now?

We can, but we've already sent the search parties out. Currentide was silent. *Well, go on! Tell us about your surroundings, maybe we'll be able to send a messenger out or something.*

She tried her best to think about what her surroundings looked like.

Well, it's very gray. Yesterday we followed a dark path and fell asleep on it last night. It was very hard and uncomfortable. When my friends and I awoke, there were people in these objects traveling all around us. They went pretty fast and were gray as well. We're now traveling above it using air.

Currentide figured it was best for the moment not to tell her parents they were headed in the direction everyone else was traveling away from.

Peculiar… her parents replied. *Well, tell us when something changes.*

Will do, boss, thought Currentide. The contact ceased.

"How long do you think we'll be traveling today?" Stratus asked around midday of no one in particular.

Pyra stared at the horizon for some minutes. "I don't know. Back in the kingdoms, I know our towns weren't evenly spaced. It could be days before we reach something. If we find a place similar to where we were being kidnapped, I say we rest there for the night. I do not want to wake up near those horrid things again."

She shivered at the memory.

"Places like that are too far away from the path. We need to stay nearby this path, lest we be completely lost."

"Oh, yeah? What makes you so sure of that?"

"Well, considering our distance from the horizon, we should reach a town by nightfall."

"Huh?"

All but Stratus squinted toward the horizon. There was a small dot one could possibly call a town. They were silent for most of the rest of the trip as they slowly gained on the oncoming town.

As they approached it, they found themselves feeling as if it should have a name other than "town." It was simply very large, and none of them had ever seen a town quite as big. However, there was no word in their vocabulary to describe this sight, so this proved to be a problem.

Just as the girls were starting to feel drowsy from that day's events, Stratus landed them just outside of the town's limits. The princesses awoke with a jolt as they hit the hard ground.

"What was that for?" Pyra demanded, beginning to flare up. "A little warning would have been nice, or you could have slowly set us down. Is it so hard to be mindful of others?"

"Well, it's winter, so yes," Stratus replied with a smile similar to that of a child who knows he is in trouble.

Pyra groaned and pulled at what little hair she had. "Let's just go inside the town-thing and find a place to rest for the night."

At this point, the people-object-things had almost no traffic. Nonetheless, the princesses chose to walk beside the path rather than on it. They did not want a repeat of that morning.

As the princesses walked into town, they stared with saucer eyes at all the sights. Stratus tried to look unimpressed, but she couldn't suppress her awe. Compared to the towns in their kingdoms, this place was huge. There were buildings larger than the castles and bright lights everywhere. It reminded Pyra of home in a strangely chilling way; Stratus was perfectly fine. Currentide and Petunia took a few minutes to adjust to the brightness. It was a similar experience to that of when they first saw their kidnappers, and the light was behind David.

They walked slowly as they stared. Even though there were bright lights, the town was nonetheless very gray. They wondered how people could call this place home, but the residents here could very well say the same about the princesses' homes. The air was also very smoky, musty, and humid. All but Pyra gagged upon entering. Stratus and Petunia were used to a much cleaner air from high up or caused by plants. The polluted air seeped into Currentide's water, thus making it hard for her to breathe as well.

How is this air not bothering you? Currentide sent to Pyra, for it was hard to breathe and harder to speak.

"Um, obviously fire has smoke coming from it," she answered. "Ha, I could get used to this place. The lights and smoke remind me in a dark way of home, but hey, let's find a place to stay the night."

Pyra took the lead in their search for rest. The others squinted, trying to lessen the sting of the putrid air. Tears were welling up, making it that much harder. From what Petunia could see, the writing in this town was similar to the books she read when they were kidnapped. Then, she got an idea.

"Hey...Stratus," she said in between coughs. "Do any... of these...words look familiar to you?"

Petunia started to have a little fit of coughs, which was an easy accomplishment.

Stratus tried to open her eyes up some. "Yeah, but I... still don't know...what it says...dummy."

Petunia looked down and continued to follow Pyra. They walked for a few minutes, with the occasional object whizzing by.

"Hey, guys?" Pyra said as she stopped and turned around. The princesses continued to cough. Pyra was forced to talk over them. "How about staying here for the night?"

Since she was now facing them, she gestured behind her and to the left. There was a bright large sign that read, "*Letoh! Emoc yats htiw su dna evas a eldnub fo ruoy suoicerp hsac!*" There was a picture containing a bed similar to the ones in the place they were kidnapped and a tankard of rum.

The princesses looked up at the very tall and narrow building.

"I'm not...sure," coughed Stratus. "It...looks dodgy."

"Oh, c'mon!" Pyra retaliated. Fire started to form on her exterior. "It's got a picture of a bed. Surely, that means we can rest for the night?"

"Mmmm. I don't know."

"Well, I'm going to stay here tonight, and you can go find your own place to stay."

Pyra began stepping toward the building. Petunia and Currentide quickly followed, not wanting to be left behind.

"Hey! Don't leave me! It's not the summer. I'm not *that* prideful!"

Stratus jogged to catch up with them. When they arrived at the door, Pyra moved her hand toward it as if to grab a handle that wasn't there when the door slid open. The girls jumped back, and the door closed itself. The princesses looked at each other, wondering what other strange things this town might have. They stepped toward it once more, and it opened yet again. They slowly proceeded, and the door closed behind them.

Inside was an even stranger sight. They saw many people sitting around, laughing, drinking, and holding some strange objects in their mouths. Smoke would emit from their mouths when the object was taken out. All the people were inside the strange projectiles they'd seen earlier. Little mobile arms allowed them to do most of the previously described actions.

The princesses searched for someone who might be in charge when a small something floated toward them. It was boxy and had arms but no legs. It was about the length and height of the dictionary the girls had earlier but was thinner. There was a screen with a face. It looked like the thing Natascha held in her hands sometimes.

"Hello," it said. "How may I be of service for you today?"

The girls were taken aback once more. Petunia answered for them.

"Um, we would simply like to stay the night, if you will, please," she said with a curtsy. One could never be too polite. Currentide clumsily followed suit, having never performed a curtsy before.

"Scanning," it said once more. A bright light shone upon their bodies. "Will the room on the screen be suitable to your needs? Please tap the desired answer."

On the screen there was a front area with four doors leading off into its own bedroom, bathroom, and closet. Petunia looked at the others and touched the green square rather than the red one. Both had words on them, but of course she didn't understand them. She picked green because it reminded her of home.

"Ready to teleport," the thing said.

"Wait, what?" Stratus questioned.

She was too late. The teleportation had already begun when she asked the question. The princesses began to dematerialize. They felt a strange, tickling sensation. They also felt really lost and confused, as if they were missing something. They rematerialized in the room that had been shown on the screen previously. The flying object was no longer with them.

Each of the girls had a slight headache.

"I never want to do that again," complained Stratus.

"For once," Pyra said, "I agree with you, but I mean we have a place to stay for a night, right?"

"Um, guys?" Currentide said. "I don't think there's a door leading to the outside. I've checked all four, and they each lead to a bedroom, just like that thing showed us."

Petunia looked away.

"I'm sorry," she apologized. "It's my entire fault. I was the one who spoke with it and agreed to have this room. Now, we're stuck again."

Before Petunia could start crying badly, Pyra spoke up.

"Hey, it's not going to kill us to stay in weird beds for a night rather than on a hard path. Let's all just get some sleep while we can. We'll need to leave early again, so we can get home as soon as possible."

"Early *again*?" Stratus echoed. "Girl, I don't know about you, but I like my sleep!"

"Which would you rather have?" Pyra snapped. "A good night's rest or to be back in your kingdom?"

Stratus paused for a moment as she considered. Pyra shook her head and headed toward a room.

"I was kidding!" Stratus made a futile attempt. She sighed and headed toward a room herself. She might as well get sleep while she could.

"Well," said Currentide. "I guess, good night."

Petunia smiled. "See you in the morning. Bright and early!"

They left to go to bed as well. The kidnapping in addition to their journey was taking its toll on the group.

Pyra had automatically taken on the leadership position since Currentide was figuring some things out, Stratus changed too often, and Petunia was too soft for such a job. It was starting to stress Pyra out. She didn't like having to take care of the others; Petunia could probably be given that job without her knowing since she did it most of the time anyway.

Before Currentide went to bed, she thought about all that had happened that day, hoping her parents were tuning in, which they did. They would occasionally stop her for clarification, and Currentide did the best she could. This foreign land had too many strange things she didn't understand. It was too unfamiliar, and she wanted to get out as soon as possible.

Petunia wanted to get something accomplished, but her body was too exhausted to do anything more than sleep. She had entered her room all cheery, but as soon as she sat on her bed, her body started moving on its own. Rather than sitting upright, it slowly eased into lying down. The second she closed her eyes, she fell into a deep sleep.

Stratus wanted to figure some things out before she went to bed. There was an object on one wall similar to the one which "teleported" them not too long ago. This object didn't have arms and was larger by far. Stratus feared detaching it. She walked up to it, wondering if it could do anything useful for her. She tapped it, and it sprang to life. Stratus took a few steps back to survey it effectively.

"How may I be of assistance?" it asked. It had the same face as the other thing.

"How do I get to the Air Kingdom from here?" she asked. She waited a few minutes as it hummed. "Well?"

"I cannot find anything containing the words 'Air Kingdom.' Is there something else you would like me to do?"

Stratus glared at it. "Nothing? Well then, please tell me where I am currently at on a map displaying all the kingdoms."

The thing hummed again, this time producing an answer, which replaced its face.

A map was being displayed of two areas of land, one being named the Latem Kodgink and the other being the Ygolonhcet Kodgink. There was a white, blinking dot in the Ygolonhcet Kodgink. All the towns in the Ygolonhcet Kodgink were evenly spaced apart. The dot was on a town called Nitram Ts. There was no Air, Fire, Water, or Earth Kingdom on the map anywhere.

"You stupid thing!" Stratus yelled, the others could not hear her, for the walls were thick. "I told you to show me a map of the kingdoms!"

She kicked the object on the wall. She did no damage to it; however, it hurt her feet. After that, she simply decided to go to sleep, all the while muttering about these stupid things.

29

Crash

Petunia, who had awakened first, spent time with the object in her room, trying to figure out how they were to leave the room.

"Excuse me," she said, "thing on the wall?"

It sprang to life and had the same face as the one in Stratus's room.

"How may I be of assistance?" it asked.

"Well, first of all I would like to know what to call you."

"Like all computers, I am called George. My model is the Luvo 5000 Refos Edition 27."

"Thank you thus far, George. If you don't mind I have a few more questions. How are my friends and I to get out of this room?"

The image switched from a face to the front room, displaying how to leave.

"In the front room, there is a compartment. To open the compartment, you must pull out using the handle. Inside the compartment, a scanner will come out requiring each of your individual fingerprints, eye prints, and a strand of DNA. Your payments will be charged to their respective accounts."

The image showed an attractive couple demonstrating how to do these things.

"Thank you, George. Your assistances are no longer required. I do hope you get paid well for this job."

George simply shut himself off. After this, Petunia went to the front room where she waited for the others to wake up and arrive. Once everyone was there, Petunia opened the compartment, which was exactly where the image showed it to be. Petunia proceeded to explain how they were to "scan" their fingers and eyes as well as provide a piece of DNA.

"And after that we have to provide something called DNA, although I'm not sure what that is, but George showed pictures of hair, blood samples, as well as saliva so I'm assuming those all contain 'DNA.'"

Stratus gave her a look after everyone else had been scanned and given DNA.

"Do you *really* expect me to do this silly nonsense with the rest of you?"

"Are you saying you have a better plan to get out of here?" Currentide challenged, tired of hearing comments like this from Stratus, although she knew why Stratus said them.

"Well, we could easily knock the walls down. I mean, c'mon, we're princesses for crying out loud! With our powers combined, we can escape quickly."

"As much as I like the idea of destroying the walls," said Pyra, "I think Petunia's way is the easiest. I don't know about you, but I'm tired of fighting. I want a break."

"I can't believe you've changed this much. Had I asked you months ago, you would have been all for this plan, and now look at you. You're being rational and logical, and since it's winter, I don't like it."

"Well, you can break down the walls or ceiling or whatever, and we can actually get out of here and go home."

Stratus stood there for some time before giving in to the scanning and giving, mumbling about it all the while. Once she had finished, a door materialized in the front room. The princesses looked at one another then opened it. It surprisingly led back to where they had entered last night. They proceeded to exit their room and enter back out into the mucky atmosphere, where they coughed much once more. There was much more traffic outside now that it was daytime.

"I say—" started Stratus, but was stopped by a coughing fit.

Currentide saw what she was going to say and sent it to Pyra.

She wants to go above all this smoke and continue riding the air until we get to another town.

Pyra nodded. *Fair enough*, she thought, not caring whether Currentide was listening in or not. *I don't think we can stand this atmosphere much longer, so we might as well get away from it as fast as we can.*

"Stratus," she said. "Take us away."

Stratus's face lit up, glad to hear they could get some fresher air. The others were grateful too. As soon as Stratus took them away from all the smoke and pollution, the quartet could breathe once more. They rode off to the side of the path since their first concern was getting away from the town. This way, the path was still in sight, and if the next town was anything like this one, they would be far enough away, the air there wouldn't attack their lungs.

There was one thing about this place that only struck Petunia as odd. There were no plants here. It was making Petunia very melancholy, although the others were too caught up in their own agendas to notice any change in Petunia. If any of them thought anything about it, they figured she was caught up in her thoughts as well.

And so the princesses sat in silence for hours as they traveled. Nothing much happened, and they passed nothing interesting. It was the same stretch for miles. Finally, Petunia wanted to break the silence. She needed something to keep her mind off the lack of plants lest she wanted to go into a depression.

"Hey, girls," she said, and all heads turned toward her. "I was wondering… Do you think we could ask people for help in the next town? I don't like these…computers named George. I think it will be much more effective to ask a person and, if we can, read books to find maps."

Pyra nodded. "I agree. Let's do that once we reach the next town."

At one point during all of this, Currentide continued listening, but she also looked off into the distance, hoping to sight *something* different and interesting. She spotted a flying object that she couldn't identify. It was rounded and had wings on both sides. She stared at it as it came closer very quickly. It resembled a fish to Currentide in a somewhat odd way. It was moving at an alarming pace. She keyed in on Stratus's thoughts; Stratus didn't appear to have noticed it. Currentide waited to see if she would ever notice it. When it came too close for comfort, Currentide sent a message.

Watch out! she said.

Stratus immediately started paying attention, but she saw it too late. All four of the princesses were hit by it. They clutched onto the wings, knowing if they fell, it was most likely only Stratus would live.

This is what the obstacle courses were training us for! Currentide sent to the other three. *Except now we can use our powers! Simply think of it as the obstacle course of air.*

After receiving the message, they tried different things. Pyra climbed to the top, searing hand- and footholds into the body of the vehicle. There, she easily stood; it reminded her of riding Stratus's air. Stratus had already jumped off and now flew alongside it. Currentide, seeing Stratus, made Stratus want Currentide to fly with her. Stratus proceeded to widen the fast air, and Currentide jumped on.

Petunia, however, wondered if the object was flying, surely there were people inside. The element known as earth was not very useful in the air, so she simply dangled for some time, wondering where she should go and how.

Currentide, who had been listening in on the others' thoughts, made Stratus look around the flying object for some sort of entryway. Currentide had the fear that if she didn't make Stratus do things, Stratus wouldn't do them of her own free will. She found a door-shaped area and sent Petunia a message.

I've found a door on the other side of the vehicle. If you can get to where Pyra climbed up, then you and Pyra can jump onto the air with Stratus and me. Pyra can open the door with fire, and we can all enter.

Petunia nodded. She attempted to slide over to where Pyra had landed earlier. Her foot slipped at one point, and she dangled there. Using what little upper arm strength she had, she somehow managed to pull her body up, so her foot was balancing on the wing-looking thing. Soon enough, she was at the foot- and handholds Pyra had created. She climbed up much more easily.

When she reached the top, she tried to tell Pyra the plan, but the wind was too noisy. Currentide sent Pyra the plan, to which she agreed. Currentide told Petunia Pyra already knew the plan. The two jumped off the yet-to-be-identified flying object and onto the air Stratus was controlling. Petunia didn't land quite right, and Currentide had to help pull her back up.

They approached the door, where Pyra scorched it right off. They went closer toward the entrance, and Petunia jumped in easily, rolling to the other side. The others came in as she was standing up and dusting herself off. Currentide released her control over Stratus once they were inside.

"What in the world just happened?" she questioned. "I was just outside controlling the air, and now I'm inside. I remember what happened, but I don't recall making the choices whatsoever. Currentide! Did you do this to me? I know people from the Water Kingdom can control minds. I've read books on the subject."

Currentide was content with not replying. Petunia explored the space in an attempt to find a person who would hopefully give them some useful information to find their way to their respective homes. When she entered the cockpit, she found two people. She smiled a sigh of relief, pronouncing her features all the more.

"Oh, thank goodness," she said quietly and without meaning to, then with more determination to be heard. "Hello, my name is Petunia. My friends and I entered your, um, vehicle, and were wondering if you would please help us?"

Neither one of them answered her. Petunia's face fell for a second. She didn't want to force them, but they really should be getting home.

"Excuse me?" she said. She tapped one on the shoulder. He jumped and turned around.

Now she was able to get a good look at the strange projectiles they'd seen on the dark line and at the inn. It resembled a chair without legs. It appeared as if something large and round was on top it with four limbs dangling out. A flat device with many keys strapped in front. A large head was at the top, and a clear bubble covered the front of the projectile.

He looked over at his co-pilot and typed a short sentence. Petunia cocked her head in confusion; the co-pilot didn't awake. He jumped as his chair spoke to him with George's voice.

"You have an incoming message," it said. "'Um, there's a girl in our cockpit.'"

The co-pilot's eyes widened when he finally saw Petunia. Petunia smiled, glad to see they had noticed her and could very possibly help her now.

"Oh, good!" she exclaimed, unable to contain her happiness. She shook their hands. "Once again I'd like to tell you my name is Petunia. Oh, so much has happened, and I can't tell you all of it in this short amount of time, but long story short, my friends and I were kidnapped, and we kind of ended up hitting your vehicle. We're safely inside now. Oh, I didn't think to even ask if it was all right. Silly me. It is, isn't it?"

She awaited with curious eyes for an answer. The two men simply sat with wide eyes at this beautiful girl. They had never seen anyone quite like this. They weren't sure how to react.

One of them typed, "George, what does protocol say to do when we hit a girl, and she enters our cockpit?"

He waited a minute before George answered him aloud.

"There is nothing pertaining to this matter," it said.

The pilot looked at his co-pilot, who did his best to shrug.

"I found her!" said a voice from outside the cockpit.

Petunia looked behind her. Her friends were coming this way. She turned around.

"Gentlemen, if you wouldn't mind, I would like to introduce you to my friends."

She walked out of the cockpit. After a few minutes of indecision of how to proceed, the pilots exited their piloting station. The station still had many button and gears, but neither pilot knew what any of them did. The plane was always kept on autopilot. If something happened, they consulted George, who usually solved whatever problem had arisen for them. Their eyes grew very wide once they saw the other girls on their plane. They all looked so...odd.

"Gentlemen," said Petunia. "I'd like to introduce you to my friends. This is Pyra, Stratus, er, Cirrus, and Currentide."

Pyra waved politely, hoping they could get home faster this way. This projectile seemed to move quickly. Stratus was glaring at Petunia for using her actual name. Her arms were crossed, and she looked as if she was having the most dreadful time. Currentide smiled shyly, unsure how to feel about these two men. She felt much better now that she could read the minds of everyone around her. It was a relief; however, she couldn't help but wonder why she couldn't read the minds of her kidnappers.

"Might we get to know your names?" Petunia questioned.

Both of the men tapped a few buttons on their chairs. Their names resounded from somewhere.

"Michael, Resident 005278039 of Sector 8."

"Antonio, Resident 00359481 of Sector 27."

Petunia nodded as if she completely understood. "Oh, okay. Thank you."

Before Petunia could continue, her comrade could not contain herself. Before Antonio and Michael had come out, Petunia, Pyra, and Currentide agreed it was best to be as kind as possible. However, this was a great problem for

Stratus since it was not spring. She tried to say nothing, but the urge was too great to resist.

And so, Cirrus stopped Petunia abruptly, and it came flowing right out of her mouth.

"So who's who?" she questioned. "Do you really think we would know which one you are? C'mon, it's obvious we're not locals. All those numbers mean nothing to us. And do you guys have a problem with actually talking to us? It makes sense for those of the Water Kingdom to not talk since they can communicate with their minds. So is there some kind of power or ability you guys have? Natascha and David weren't very clear about anything. How can you sit there with your mouth wide open? You're drooling—gross! And what in the world is the 'Igolonchet Mojinka' or 'Latame Mojinka?' Ah, what am I doing, I don't even know how to say those words properly. I just wish all the stupid people in this forsaken place could actually give us some answers. Has *anybody* ever heard of the word hospitality? And besides, the way I've been treated so far is no way to treat a princess, and—"

"Cirrus!" Pyra demanded, fire beginning to form on her exterior. Earlier, the group had agreed not to mention they were princesses, in case everyone in this land was against them and were ordered to recapture them.

Currentide looked down at the ground. She hadn't stopped Stratus from saying it, and she could have. She was focusing more on the few thoughts of Antonio and Michael.

I'm sorry, she sent to the others. *I have failed you.*

Petunia sighed and decided the plan was gone, and they should just plow on with this new information they'd given.

"Yes," she said. "We're actually princesses. We didn't want to tell you because we feared you would contact our captors, and they would kidnap us once more."

Without meaning to, Petunia activated her sappy eyes, which are practically irresistible—not many can say no to them. Petunia has yet to realize the full potential of those eyes and what they could do for her.

"We just want to get back home, and if you could please help us, that would be most wonderful. We would greatly appreciate it, and I promise we'll give you something in return for all of your help."

"Helping the—" was as far as Stratus got before Currentide shut her off, not wanting to fail her friends again. Stratus had been planning to mumble. "Helping the princesses should be reward enough."

"So will you help us?" Pyra asked, prompting their answer.

Michael and Antonio began typing swiftly at their keyboards. The princesses weren't entirely sure what was happening, but they hoped for the best.

As they stood there, their anxiety rose, awaiting an answer. The only sounds were the whirring of the engine, the princesses' heartbeats, and the tip-tapping of the pilots' flying fingers. Finally, they came up with an answer.

"We will help you," George's voice came from somewhere, "But we must know your resident and sector numbers, so we can report them."

30

A Plane Ride

"We also will need to know where we are supposed to be headed."

Petunia's face fell.

"You see," she said, "we don't have…resident or sector numbers. We're not even sure where we're at."

"Actually," Cirrus said. "We're in some place called the Igolonchet Mojinka, or something like that."

Antonio got an idea. "If you saw it, would you recognize it? Or maybe you could type it in?"

He gestured toward his keyboard and screens. Stratus wanted to laugh at their ignorance.

"Of course, I would remember it," she clipped.

She walked toward him and stared at the odd keys. Using her index fingers, she poked the squares to form the words she wanted. Antonio's face brightened up.

"I thought that's what you meant by whatever it was you said earlier. You see, you're in a place called the Technology Kingdom. Our neighbor is the Metal Kingdom. Is that where you're from?"

Petunia shook her head, confused. "No, we've never heard of such kingdoms before."

Michael's face became troubled. "Then where are you from?"

One by one the princesses named off their kingdoms, pronouncing them proudly. The pilots began searching these kingdoms they'd never heard of, asking how to spell them. Their searches were futile. The princesses looked at the maps after several minutes of waiting. For Stratus, it was all very familiar since she'd looked at it the night before.

"Do you have any parchment or inkwells on this…um, what is it called again?" Petunia asked.

Stratus sighed. "It's called a plane, Petunia. Seriously, why can't you remember a few words?"

Petunia looked at the ground.

"No," one of the pilots answered after a search. "We do not have the skin of sheep, goats, etc., prepared for use as a material on which to write with a small container for ink."

Petunia sighed. Currentide, reading her thoughts, thought of an alternative route to accomplish Petunia's goal.

"Is there a way we could draw on something?" Currentide asked. "Petunia wanted to draw a map, so we could show you how our kingdoms look on a map. We might be able to piece them together and get a general idea of where we might need to be headed."

The pilots nodded. Michael went to the cockpit and ordered his chair to pick up the old tablets. He came back with them in his lap and handed them to the princesses so they could all draw a version of the map. They explained what they were and how to use them. They thought it was better to have multiple versions rather than one. This way, each kingdom would have one closest resembling itself since there was one person from each of these unheard of places. Once the princesses were finished, they handed the tablets back, and the pilots transferred the data onto one giant screen. The girls watched from behind and beside the chairs.

Since half of the Four Kingdoms were islands, the pilots tried to place them over the islands surrounding the Metal Kingdom. This was to no avail. No borders looked like they would match up almost precisely.

"There must be a gap of some sort between the Technology and Metal Kingdoms and the Four Kingdoms," said Petunia, using the common term to group the Fire, Water, Earth, and Air Kingdoms.

"Way to state the obvious," said Stratus with a roll of the eyes. "Of course they don't match up, Petunia. They're *islands*."

Petunia was silent once more to a comment from Stratus. She knew if she was patient, this storm of winter would expire. When spring came, Stratus would be happy, and all would be well, but for now, Petunia knew she must deal with these dreadful comments. This, too, would pass, just like the kidnapping did.

"Well," Michael asked via George, "what if we just flew really high and see if we recognized anything?"

The princesses looked at each other and shrugged.

"It's not like we have much else to do," Pyra replied.

The pilots nodded.

"It's settled, then. We'll start looking after we drop our cargo off."

The girls smiled, glad to finally have more of a plan rather than "Let's fly and ask around." They knew this would be much faster than Stratus's air, much to her disagreement. And so the princesses sat on a plane until that evening when the pilots had finished unloading. Petunia wanted to help unload, but the pilots deemed that as silly and thought it was best for the princesses to come into contact with as little amount of people as possible.

As soon as the cargo, engines of all sorts, was unloaded, the pilots reentered the plane and smiled at the princesses.

"Don't you worry," Michael said as Antonio closed the new entrance hatch, considering the old one was destroyed with fire. "We'll get you home safe as soon as we can."

"Can we find the Air Kingdom first?" Stratus asked. "You know, it's in the sky and all. I figured it would be the easiest."

She shrugged. They had yet to take off since they weren't quite sure which direction they were going.

"I guess it's okay," said Currentide. Pyra agreed.

"Sure, let's do that," she said but added in her head. *The sooner you get home, the less we'll have to deal with your nasty comments.*

"I'll be fine to get home last," said Petunia. "I want to make sure the rest of you get home safely, or else I'll worry my head off."

Pyra and Currentide laughed since they knew the truth of her words, and Petunia couldn't help but crack a smile.

Antonio nodded.

"Cirrus, if you'll come with me, maybe we can work some kind of sense of direction out."

She followed silently for once. In the cockpit, the two looked at maps and decided to coast along the border of the Technology Kingdom and away from the Metal Kingdom. They planned to be twenty thousand kilometers in the air for the best possible vantage point the vehicle could handle without dying a horrible death. Once all was decided, Stratus went outside of the cockpit to get Michael. The three of them would be sitting up there, Stratus mainly to keep an eye on them and make sure they were going where they were supposed to. She sat, criticizing them for not knowing how to use the plane until they took off.

The flight began before they knew it since it was such a smooth takeoff. The princesses were glad they were finally going to go home. The girls quickly fell asleep, as did the pilots. The plane flew on autopilot commanded by George whose instructions were to coast the border, and if anything strange appeared, to sound the alarm.

A couple hours after midnight, the alarm sounded. It immediately awoke Petunia and the pilots. Currentide awoke to them screaming in their minds as well as out loud. Pyra and Stratus were too tired to have noticed any change in the atmosphere.

Quickly, the pilots commanded the alarm to go off. Currentide dragged Cirrus's and Pyra's bodies off to the side while Petunia ran to the cockpit.

"What did George see?" she asked frantically in the hopes they were approaching one of the Four Kingdoms.

The pilots tried to figure out what was going on.

"I'm not sure," Antonio answered as both pilots tried to figure it out. "He's not sure what he saw, so we're reviewing the footage, but it's not clearing anything up. Here, take a look."

At this moment, Currentide entered the tiny space as well and watched the recap. It was a very dark image, but they could pick shapes out. Petunia looked at Currentide, worry obvious on her face although she tried to hide it.

It's them, she thought. *How? When did they start following us? How long has this been going on? Oh, we need to wake the others up. I wonder if Currentide's been reading my mind. Oh, hurry up! You need the others up, so we can formulate a plan as a group.*

Currentide was indeed listening. Petunia hurried out to wake Pyra and Stratus. Once Cirrus was awake, Currentide stepped out of the cockpit to allow Stratus in.

"Could you show me what George found?" Cirrus asked the pilot. Antonio obliged wordlessly.

Once the video was finished, Stratus thanked them and left to go plan with the others.

All four were awake now.

"I've reviewed what George found," Cirrus told the other three princesses. "It is most definitely Natascha and David. I'd recognize that vehicle anywhere."

The others' faces went white.

"How did they find us?" Currentide whispered almost inaudibly. "I can't go back. You guys can't let us go back."

Petunia tried to put a comforting arm around her. Pyra sighed.

"Okay, we've escaped twice, only one of those times being successful," she said. "We're *not* going back, not on my time. Now, the next question is our course of action toward them. I want to see what you guys say. Do you think we should stay inside and wait it out, hoping it's just coincidence and that they just pass by? Maybe wait for them to make the first move. Or do we want to attack, pronouncing that no, we won't be captured again. We refuse and will fight to the death for our freedom? I'm all ears for opinions or other ideas."

"We have to show them who's boss!" Stratus practically shouted, back to her old winter self. The others shushed her to no avail. "I say we stand and fight, never backing down! They haven't learned their lesson to never mess with princesses. We need to teach them how powerful we are, and why they chose the wrong people to mess with. We will prevail!"

Pyra nodded at Cirrus's answer. Currentide, however, had a different viewpoint.

"I actually think we should just wait," she said. "Maybe they *aren't* going to attack us. Maybe they don't know we're in here. It's possible they're just driving near other vehicles to make them nervous and see which one will react. So it's possible they *want* us to attack to prove who we are. I think we should wait for them to make the first move."

Pyra nodded to this answer as well; she shifted her attention toward Petunia who had yet to answer. All three girls began staring expectantly toward the princess from the Earth Kingdom whose people were supposedly known for their great wisdom.

"I need some time to think," she said and walked over to a corner and paced, weighing their options and deciding which she deemed the wisest and overall the best decision.

After several minutes, Stratus grew impatient.

"Well?" she asked, obviously annoyed. "What do you think we should do, oh, wise one?"

Petunia sighed, knowing there was little time left. "What do we have to work with again?"

Pyra took her to the closet and showed her the items. There was a wilted flower in a pot, a fork with a plate to dine upon, another book no one could read, a toothbrush, a uniform of some sort, and a latex makeup kit.

"All right," she said, "I've come up with a plan, but I'm not sure if you will like it or not."

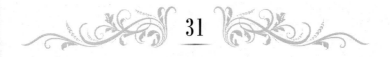

31

The Return

"You've got to be kidding me," said Stratus once they were in their positions and about to proceed with the plan. "No, absolutely not. There's no way I'm going through with this."

"Oh, c'mon!" Petunia coaxed. "Please do it. Without you performing this part, the plan will never work. We need you to do this for us. Please."

The hope in her eyes was too great for Cirrus to say no.

"Oh, fine! But I'm only doing it because I want to go home, so I can be rid of you, crazy people."

"Oh, thank you, thank you, thank you, thank you, thank you!" she said whilst squeezing Stratus tightly.

"Le…go…omme…"

"Oh, sorry." Petunia let go and tucked her hair behind her ear. "I didn't mean hurt you."

"Well, that thing nearly killed me!"

"Oh no! Please forgive me!"

"Um…Petunia, I didn't mean it was *literally* going to kill me…I just…uh…"

Petunia! Stratus! Currentide called. *We're going to start soon!*

Petunia smiled and grabbed a hold of the ladder as the plane flew high once more. She began her ascent since she and Stratus were on the ground.

Before all this, Currentide had turned off some of Stratus's senses and taken over her thought process. During this, Petunia had placed her in the greenish-gray uniform, which was much too large for her. A helmet was also strapped to her head. With the makeup Pyra had placed upon her, the Fire Kingdom is notorious for their artistic skills, she almost looked like a pilot. The only thing missing was the object the Technology Kingdom's people sat in. Luckily, one of the pilots had given them his thing to use. At this point, Petunia brought the flower back to life and created a chair for him to sit in. It took all three of the conscious girls to take him out of the thing and into Petunia's chair. Petunia was still saddened that a person was still stuck inside part of the projectile, though.

Now, Stratus used the projectile, which was more like a chair, to lower herself to ground level. The plane still flew overhead, continuing its course as if nothing had happened. She slowly moved toward the vehicle she easily recognized. The fork and dinner plate sat upon her lap.

Upon reaching the vehicle, she managed to get the chair to tap the window. She was thankful she received the tutorial earlier. The window rolled down. Both vehicles were still moving.

"Yes, pilot?" Natascha, who was driving, asked.

Stratus typed quickly, having caught on fast to the chair and its ways.

"You have given my co-pilot and me reasons to believe you are suspicious characters," it said for her which she deemed silly beyond reason.

"May I inquire these reasons?"

"Ma'am, with all due respect, you've been following our plane without contact for hours."

"Maybe I'm just going the same route as you."

"You're not on the highway." This was a new word for Stratus, but she managed to use it correctly. "I'm going to need your resident and sector numbers."

The vehicle surged forward quickly. Stratus zoomed after it, wondering if Natascha had seen through the disguise or not. The vehicle went under the ladder, which hung from the plane a few feet above it. Pyra jumped off the ladder and onto the vehicle. Stratus used air to send her the dinner plate and fork.

Pyra began searing the top to make a hole into the vehicle just large enough to throw the book in. Currentide had strongly rejected the burning of a book, but Petunia sadly said it had to be done.

Pyra made the hole now faster than when they had escaped the second time. The void was complete, and Pyra dropped the burning book and some makeup inside. She also used the dish to whack their heads and set them straight. She threw the fork in for good measure, hoping it might stab one of them somehow. Pyra then sealed the top back up. She jumped off and high-fived Stratus's makeup-covered hand. The vehicle was filled with smoke, thanks to some of the highly flammable latex makeup they had placed inside. They watched as the vehicle drove away in all of its doom.

The two princesses were paying so much attention to the vehicle they didn't notice the perpetrator behind them. Quickly, a shock went throughout their bodies, and the air from their lungs was taken away. They were fighting for more, but darkness overcame them first.

Inside the plane, Currentide was holding the toothbrush.

"Now, what was I doing with this again?" she asked.

Petunia smiled, happy to help. "Is there any way you can freeze water?"

Currentide opened the hatch to see how cold it was and how fast they were going. It seemed like it would work fairly well.

"Yes," she replied upon returning. "I suppose I can."

"Well, if we can make a frozen projectile out of this—"

"Oh, I see!" Currentide interrupted, having read Petunia's thoughts to where it was going.

And so she put water around it, held the toothbrush outside, and froze it quickly. She then began to descend down the ladder. About halfway down, a shock erupted throughout her body, and she fell to the ground with a thud.

"Thank you for all your hospitality, sirs," Petunia said to the pilots who nodded. "It's been a pleasure meeting you, and maybe we'll meet again in the future. Well, it's time for me to go. We'll try our hardest to get your backing back to you, Antonio."

Petunia began her descent as well. Upon touching the ground, she waved to the plane. She turned around to face David and Natascha. Petunia hung her head.

"You're back for us, aren't you?" she whispered to the ground.

"Oh no," said Natascha sarcastically. "We've come to have tea with you this fine morning."

"Really?" Petunia's face lit up, not catching on.

Natascha's mouth was a thin line. "No. Wow, you're really gullible, aren't you?"

Petunia looked down again. The others had called her that often. She looked up at those who had captured her before, knowing she was unable to fight back.

"Do you have my friends?" she whispered almost inaudibly. They nodded. "Please don't hurt them. They're strong and wonderful people once you get to know them."

She set her wrists our before them. Tears were forming in her eyes.

"So just take me, please, so I can be with them again. They're my friends, and I cannot allow them to be captured as I run away. I will not let you treat them badly either, however. If I let you take me with no struggle, will you promise not to hurt them?"

The captors looked at each other, knowing they could simply shock her and get this all over with.

"How about…"

Natascha paused. Petunia could only wonder how the sentence would end. Natascha smiled coldly.

"No?"

Petunia's body fell limply onto the ground.

All four girls awoke to throbbing headaches. They were truly getting tired of this. All they wanted was to go home. Was that too much to ask for?

"Well, friends, I guess we're back, huh?" Currentide commented gloomily.

Pyra set her bed back on fire. She used the wall as her punching bag again. She hated being in this room. She hated getting captured *again*. She hated Natascha. She hated David. She wanted to go back home where she understood things, and all of this stress was just making her angry.

Stratus yawned loudly.

"Can't they just let us go?" she asked.

Petunia was silent. She knew her comrades wouldn't like that she gave herself over without a fight. They would be upset if they found out, so she resided in staying silent.

A knock came to their door. That was strange; no one had ever knocked before.

"Um, come in?" Petunia said questioningly.

The door opened slowly.

"Um, I was told to look for a room with four princesses in it on the third floor?"

"Well you've found us," Stratus muttered. "Four kidnapped princesses coming right up."

The other girl sighed and opened the door more, revealing who she was.

"Kidnapped? Whatever. Look, my name's Princess Latinoom of the Metal Kingdom, but call me Latty. It's nice to meet you. And what do you do for food around here? I'm starving."

ACKNOWLEDGMENTS

First and foremost, I want to thank God who has given me such wonderful talents and dreams. Without Him, I wouldn't be where I am now. I never would have dreamed this big or gotten it done. Thank You.

I'd also like to thank my parents, Greg and Hadley Tolle, for reading what they could and giving me feedback. Thank you so, so much for letting me talk through my crazy plot problems and at the very least pretend like you were listening to my ramblings. So, so many ramblings. I don't know how you managed to do it. As I've said before (and I'm positive you figured this out in my seventeen years of life), I could talk about my books forever. So I thank you for lending a listening ear.

I want to thank my big brother Spencer Tolle for being excited when you found out my book was getting published. You get so excited about a lot of things, and I hope you stay that way. Thanks for being that cool brother who brags on his sister while simultaneously makes a joke out of her. I love you! I know you love me too, even if you won't admit it.

Thank you to my editing team for allowing me to realize that my "artistic decision" was really just distracting to the reader. Thank you for opening my eyes to some big things I hadn't seen in my work previously.

Thank you to my cover design team for making a really cool book cover. It's not what I would have initially thought up, so thanks for letting me see my book from a different view. I'm glad I can have talented cover designers like you.

I want to thank my best friend Elizabeth Miller for so many things. You're one of the best friends a girl could have. I'm so glad we get to share in our weirdness together, and I'm glad God has placed you in my life. Thanks for creating worlds with me and listening to all my nonsense about writing. I'd especially like to thank you for listening to me read my manuscript (with voices) to you as I was writing it. You are the icing to my cupcake.

Thank you so much to Robin Murphy for reading the last draft of my work. Your suggestions have been really helpful. They've allowed me to see my work from a little different angle. I know they're making my book better overall, so thank you for letting me reach something I hadn't seen earlier.

Thanks so much Tate Publishing for taking on my book! I'm glad you are a part of making one of my dreams come true. You guys have been great in the publishing process. It means a lot to me that you would take on someone as young and inexperienced as me, so I thank you.

I want to thank all my teachers who have taught me English. It really comes in handy when you're writing a full-length novel.

Also, thank you to anyone who listened to me ramble on and on about my book. As I said earlier, I could talk about it forever. So if you get me started on something, it's your own fault…not really.

Thank you to everyone who purchased and/or read this book. It means a lot to me when people sound interested in this thing I've put so much time and effort into. It means even more to me when someone reads my book and thoroughly enjoys it. An author isn't much without fans, so thank you.

Keep your dreams alive!